Books in

The Human-Hybrid Project

series:

Inside the Darkness

Inside the Darkness

Farley L. Dunn

THREE SKILLET

INSIDE THE DARKNESS

Book 2 in the Series:
THE HUMAN-HYBRID PROJECT

Published in Fort Worth, Texas

 THREE SKILLET

www.ThreeSkilletPublishing.com

Three Skillet Publishing
PO Box 162194
Fort Worth, Texas 76161

ISBN: 978-1-943189-92-2

First Printing April 2021/Printed in the USA

Inside the Darkness

— Book 2 —

The Human-Hybrid Project

Corona Tower Research Complex

Basement Level 1

Underground Parking

Military Housing

Cafeteria

Offices

Tower Footprint and Main Elevator

Storage Tanks

Basement Level 2

Research Center Main Lobby

Staffing Housekeeping

Key:

1 Block

Research Labs

Garik's Quarters

Basement Level 3

Emergency Clinic

Corona City

Cafeteria

Living Space Failed Hybrids

Recreation Area

Natatorium

Sound Proof Training Cells

Storage

Cafeteria

Cages for Animals

Power Plant

Hospital

Basement Level 4

Basement Level 5

Utility Right of Way

— I —

D

arkness swirled, reaching for Garik Shayk and spinning him in a tornado of images.

Like Dorothy, he imagined, trying to focus and locate something familiar. He would rather find Marisa. He pictured his petite girlfriend, reached for her, searching for her hand, and she was gone, swallowed in the inky otherness.

He thought he glimpsed Ibn, Muhammad, and Hayat, skaters all, his friends through thick and thin. They were used to being upside down, their world catawampus, skating the streets of the city, performing their trick moves as though an adoring crowd cheered them on, prowling to brush their trucks against every curb and bench hidden by the shadows in the dead of night.

If Garik could find anyone in his tornado, they would be there.

Abruptly, he gasped, newly dizzy, and he sat up, throwing sweaty sheets and a blanket to the side, still falling, falling. He tossed his hands to his head to thrust them into his hair, only to find freshly shorn bristles covering his scalp. Reality rushed over him like a broken floodgate emptying the cesspool of his world into his head.

They had cut his *hair!*

He opened his eyes, and the falling room righted itself, shifting around him into a cohesive box of walls and windows and a floor and a ceiling. "Not Oz," he accused the room, and he released a hard breath, puffing his cheeks out, not remembering everything, but he remembered the needle.

Over and over, the needle.

What had they called it? Sleepy juice. Nurse Ratchett, er, Nurse Leah, placing the needle to his skin, and slipping it so effortlessly inside. He ran fingers down the smooth crook of the inside of his elbow. So many puncture marks. How many times had he fought back? How many times had they given him the sleepy juice? Too many times. Why? *Why?* He did grin, though, remembering one thing. The straps. It seemed he'd fought back, even if he didn't remember all of it. "Good for you, Garik," he whispered to himself. "That's showing them."

The room was cold. He tested his feet to ensure they weren't strapped down. They had been the last time he remembered anything at all. Nurse Ratchett and Dr. Strangelove, aka Dr. Jamie. He shivered at the memory. *"Do you know what you want to become?"* Then, *"We thought we had learned this lesson. We shall have to return to the straps."*

Garik's feet moved just fine, and he threw aside the bedding and drew up his knees. His ankles, the familiar bronze skin snaking out of loose, full-length pajamas in an animal print. His upper body was bare. Loosely tied cords at his waist secured the pants, and he swung his legs over the side of the bed. His toes just touched the floor, and he was surprised to find it pleasingly warm.

He pushed himself to a standing position, fully prepared to catch himself. He remembered the tornado. He must have been on something, the sleepy juice, per-haps, and it hadn't completely worn off. His thoughts felt wonky, like he was still caught up in it, and his thoughts were constantly being twisted inside out. What he wanted to find was the exit, a way out of here.

The room contained several doors, the main one closed. A darkened doorway revealed a glimpse of porcelain fixtures. He took one step toward the black space, found he was stable, and took a second.

Walking. He breathed in deeply. It felt good to walk, like he hadn't done it in a while.

He rubbed his scalp again. How long *had* it been? Too long, clearly. Inside the small bathroom, he turned on the light to reveal himself in front of a full-length mirror.

That's me? Garik wasn't sure for a moment that he was seeing himself. Then, in his aunt's apartment, the mirror over the small sink in the one tiny bathroom was postage stamp size, and when he brushed his teeth, he could barely fit in all his face at one time. Still, there were glass doors and plate glass windows around the city, and he did have pictures of himself on his watch.

Studying his shorn head and his sparse mat of newly grown hair, anger welled up in him. This wasn't the person he was supposed to be. He tightened his jaw. My mind, my reasoning, not anger. He forced himself through his self-styled mantra.

His watch! He involuntarily checked his wrist, even as he knew it was bare. All of him was, except for his borrowed pajama bottoms. They had even taken his watch, though he knew they would. How else would they keep him from calling for help from everyone he knew?

He pictured himself the last day he remembered before waking up here. He had stood in front of the flower shop doors reflected in the bright sun against the dark interior. It seemed just yesterday but was certainly weeks ago or longer. A thick, wild-boy mane of dark hair tossed into windblown disarray from his skateboard ride across the city looked back at him. He had been slim but muscular, and he was dismayed at how soft he now looked. And his *hair!* How many weeks had it been for his hair to regrow this long?

He jerked around and let his eyes roam the room, searching for clues. For anything that would give him fresh information. A bedside table with a lamp and a clock. A small desk across the room holding, and this surprised him, a computer monitor and keyboard. There was even enough space for a small sofa facing a good-size television. Across the room, the bed, rumpled, his shape still in the sheets, a slender youth of average size, revealing the impression of two arms and two legs, and yes, that was important, because he also remembered Dr. Jamie's other words: DNA. *"How's the DNA material coming along?"* And later: *"This will need to drip for a while."* Drip where? The answer was plain as orange-glow shimmer gel splashed across the walls. *Into Garik's arm.*

Who knew what that would do to his body? What had they said? Timber wolf? Garik didn't feel any different, other than frustrated from not *knowing,* from not being *told.* This was his life. They should let him know what they were doing with it.

He turned back to the mirror and moved close to

inspect himself. He lifted one eyelid and peered inside. What did wolf eyes look like? They were dogs, so there was that. Didn't some breeds have eyes of different colors? If so, his hadn't changed yet. His were still clear gray speckled with gold.

A thumb told him his teeth were still even and flat. No canine incisors to rip and tear raw flesh. His ears? Should they be pointed on top? Or was that just for werewolves? No fur on his skin, just the thin growth he was used to when he lifted his pajama legs and inspected his shins.

It seemed he was still all Garik, and that was a relief. Maybe whatever they were doing hadn't taken, and they would have to show him the door, saying, "Sorry, kid, things didn't work out. You're not the one, but then, we didn't really think you were." He could return to his small bedroom in Irina's apartment and head back to school in August. He was a senior— something he had looked forward to for three years— and while he didn't want to sit in class, he had lots of friends he missed, and he would enjoy his time with them.

"Hey," he called out. He remembered the first room, the all-white one with the wire-reinforced glass in the door. That room had spoken back to him. "Is anyone listening? I'm awake if you're there. Are your cameras on? Are you watching what I'm doing? Woo-hoo, wolf boy, waiting on instructions."

He grinned. If they were there, that would get their attention.

He checked a slim door and found a closet. The light clicked on automatically to reveal clothes, shoes, and a shelf with tees, underwear, and socks. He checked the waist of a pair of pants, and yes, they were his size, or had been before he turned all soft. Someone had been checking, doing their stuff.

The door to the room clicked, the sound of metal against metal, reminding Garik of the lock on his Street Strider when he thumbed his fob to unlock it. He stepped out of the closet to await whoever—or whatever—might be coming through the door.

THE DOOR opened wide, and a rolling metal cart with several covered items came through, followed by what Garik was relieved to see was a familiar face.

"I'm glad to see you up and moving." Nurse Leah Fortinier used her shoe to pull down a doorstop on the outside of the door. With the door secured in an open position, she worked the rest of the cart through before turning back to the door, where she wrapped one hand around the edge and released the doorstop with her foot. Before the door closed, Garik caught a short corridor and a wide doorway opening to a vast space. The exterior of the door had large letters identifying it as B2-17.

"What's that?" He nodded at the cart.

"More questions?" Leah smiled pleasantly, as she began uncovering steaming portions of food. "Now, don't expect this every day. We have a cafeteria on the first level, well, on almost every level, but you'll be expected to use the one on the first level mostly. This is because this is your first day in your new room."

Leah had moved the chair from the desk to the cart, and it now looked like a high-tech dining table on wheels.

"My room?" He wanted to say, *I have a room, and it's at City View Apartments, not this,* but he was out of his element, and he had less power here than he did when dealing with his aunt's boyfriend, Arik, meaning none at all.

"Yes. I can see you've been exploring. All those clothes are sized for you, so feel free to choose what you like."

"The weather?" He made a point of rubbing his head. "I don't know if it's even summer any longer."

"I am so sorry about that. Your hair was beautiful, but it will regrow. Don't worry about the weather. You'll be inside for the time being." She patted the back of the chair. "While it's hot?"

Garik glanced at the food. It did look good, and it smelled better. He glanced back to the closet. Clothes, yes, that would be nice, too, especially with Nurse Leah standing there watching him, as if checking on whether he had begun his transformation from normal boy to teen wolf, ready to leap across the room and bite her on the ankle.

"Okay, suit yourself." Leah didn't seem upset. "I have one question for you. Do you remember my name?"

"Nurse Ratch—" He caught himself. "I'm sorry. I mean, Nurse Leah. Fortinier is your last name."

She chuckled. "Your memory is returning. I've been Nurse Ratchett to you more times than you remember. Leah is fine. Enjoy your breakfast."

She turned to leave, and Garik stopped her.

"Leah, are you locking the door again?"

"I know you want to know everything, but you can't just yet. And we can't have you wandering the facility until you've been through orientation. There are things here—good things, we think—that need to be explained before you make up your mind."

"Will I ever be able to leave?"

"Certainly." She frowned as if surprised at the bald question. "We don't keep our project participants locked in their rooms."

"Like on the bottom floor." Garik felt his face harden, and he saw Leah wince. "I mean from this place, from all of this. Or will I wind up in prison like them?"

"Patience, Mr. Shayk. I don't have all your answers now. That's what orientation is for."

"Garik. My name is Garik." His father was Mr.

Shayk, and he lived in Russia on the other side of the world, a place Garik would be glad to be right now, even if he had been grateful to leave when he did.

"Thank you, Garik. I will remember that. For now, concentrate on breakfast and clothes."

"One more thing." This was vital. Garik had to know. "Cameras? Microphones? Is that how you knew I was up?"

This time Leah laughed. "We don't *spy* on our people, Garik. You do have your privacy, or as much as we can allow when inside your room. We do have heat sensors that tell us when you begin to move about. With our line of research, it's important to monitor body temperatures at all time. For your health, of course. Enjoy your morning, Garik. This afternoon we'll get you out and hopefully up to speed."

The door closed, too quickly for Garik to sound off another question, and yes, he listened for the thud of metal against metal. It came, solid and reinforced, if he was any judge.

Answers? Up to speed? How about out of here? That was the one and only answer he was certain he needed.

— 2 —

T

he window. Light streamed against the outside of the blinds, the casements outlined in darker patterns. Could he crawl out? If he had to.

"If it doesn't fall out of the frame and knock me out," he joked. He remembered that part of the old movie, too. "At least I can see where this place is." He imagined the upper floors of the Tower if he hadn't been moved to some distant and secretive test facility. Area 51, perhaps. He didn't see how he could scale down the side of the building, though, unless he could shimmy down the glass exterior with his bare hands and feet.

He reached to the blinds, lifted one slat, squinted, then spread it wider. Nah, it couldn't be. That was his parents' old rock house in Russia, built by his grand-papa's hands years before he was born. The wind blew, the tree he used to climb as a small boy swayed, and a bird alighted into the sky.

"What do you think, Garik, my boy?"

Garik turned, saw a face he remembered, and dropped the slat to turn completely around. He felt caught out not to have noticed the door unlocking. "About what?"

"The view." Dr. Jimenez walked fully into the room, his hands behind his back, allowing two people to follow him in. Jimenez smiled, made his way to the window, and reached to a clear rod hanging from one side. He twisted it, and the scene jumped fully into the room. Slats of sun slashed across the floor, the warmth cutting across Garik's bare feet. "Is it as you remember? Your home, that is your home out there."

"My parents' home. I live with my aunt, Irina." Still, Garik glanced out the window, squinting, hoping to see his papa and his mama, for a moment longing for their familiar faces.

"Have you forgotten?" Jimenez grasped Garik's bare shoulder in one hand, squeezed it warmly, and dipped his head to peer at him in a fatherly manner. "You have been deported. I believe Mr., um, Hefferly apprised you of your current situation." Jimenez glanced at one of his associates as he mentioned Hefferly's name, only moving on when the associate nodded.

"The black-bearded guy." Garik wanted to shrug off the doctor's hand, but he remembered Hefferly's wrist. Garik had grabbed it, twisting hard, and then he had held nothing. The man's wrist had turned to empty air, to *smoke* in his hand, before becoming real flesh once more.

Who could do that? Better, *what* could do that?

The event . . . with Hefferly on the mall . . . surely that hadn't been real, a man turning into purple smoke. That was impossible. It must have been video fakery . . . except, Garik had held his wrist, and it had *vanished* right out of his grasp.

"What about Mr. Hefferly?" Garik felt his chest tighten. Nurse Leah. Colonel Brace. The massive shoulders of Weston Rodheimer. *The needle.* And now, memories of purple smoke. His childhood home outside the window. The *tree* he had climbed as a child.

"You were deported because you broke into our secured facilities. Do you remember that?" Jimenez wasn't unkind with his words, more as though he wished to prod Garik's memories.

Garik looked back through the window, the hand on his arm keeping him connected to this room, and his thoughts flew backwards to a childhood storm. He had huddled in his bed in his room under the eaves, and lightning had punched through his small window. The crack of thunder had shaken him off his mattress, and he had fallen to the floor and rolled under the bed, pulling his blanket in after him. The next morning, the top of the old tree lay on the ground, a gaping wound in the branches, a reminder that the fist of God could strike anywhere, even just outside your window if you weren't careful.

The old tree had never been the same.

"That's not real." Garik cut a glance to the doctor, and before the man could stop him, he reached through the blinds and rapped the surface of the "window."

"Now, don't do that." Jimenez pulled him back. He grasped both his shoulders and studied Garik's face. "That was a very quick interpretation of your surroundings, and with no explanations. I didn't expect to see adaptations in you so quickly."

"Adaptations? What's that supposed to mean?" Garik shrugged off the doctor's hands. "Leah said I'd have my privacy. Can you people maybe give me some? I want to get dressed."

Garik's hope for escape was crushed. It was not a window. He wasn't in the Tower, then. Not in Russia, either. Not . . . what did he mean, adaptations? In the mirror earlier—what had he seen that Garik had missed?

"Mr. Shayk, let me—"

"Garik. I told Nurse Leah that. Do you people listen?" Garik trembled inside with frustration. He wanted to yell at the man, *Let me out of this place,* but the needle, he didn't want that again.

"Ah, yes, Garik. I will do well to remember. Let me introduce my associates, well, soon to be your associates, also, as we're making excellent progress in your case. Mr. Rodheimer is very, very pleased." Jimenez didn't seem taken aback by Garik's outburst, and he slipped an arm loosely over his shoulders and prompted him away from the window. "We can let you dress if that would make you more comfortable, but names, that won't take but a minute. First, T'Wana. T'Wana will be your physical therapist. T'Wana?"

"Hello, Garik." A woman with big features and a pronounced jaw who carried more weight than she seemed comfortable with stepped forward, offering her hand. "T'Wana Dolalas."

"Hello." When Jimenez squeezed his shoulder and nudged him forward, Garik held out his hand. "How are you?"

"I'm glad to meet you, Garik." She took his hand and gave it a squeeze, almost as if she were testing his grip, before releasing him.

"Why do I need a physical therapist? I'm fine."

T'Wana smiled, but it was Dr. Jimenez who answered. "Fine, now, my boy," and his hand squeezed Garik's shoulder reassuringly, "but the future, well, who knows? We want to keep you fine as you progress in the program. And next we have Van. Van will soon be a regular in your day. Van?"

The second person stepped forward. He wasn't old, but older than Garik—a regular adult—with good hair but a rough, pocketed face. His skin was darker than Garik's. His shirt flexed as he moved, and Garik wondered what he did, martial arts, bodybuilding, or what? He decided not martial arts, because Kevin wasn't bulky like that.

Kevin! He had been in the Tower with them when Garik and Marisa disappeared into the basement. It was a needle in his heart. He liked Kevin, felt attracted to someone who had instantly treated him as a friend, like he was important, and even invited him to take lessons at Ai Kee! Now he wished he'd had the chance to take him up on that offer.

"Garik, are you with us?" The doctor gave his shoulder a gentle reminder, a quick pump of his hand against his arm.

Garik shook his head, wiping the fog of longing from his thoughts, to see a hand reaching out to him.

"Van, Van Hermoso. I'm glad to meet you, Garik. I'll be your occupational therapist."

"I don't have an occupation." Garik took the man's hand. "Other than high school, but that's not really an occupation."

Van chuckled. "I'm here to help you develop your

occupation, or, rather, the skills you will discover in the coming months. I'll also help you maintain what you already have. No sense in letting those go to waste." He released Garik's hand and stepped back, his movements quick, spare, and assured.

"Oh." Garik let that sink in. DNA. Timber wolf. *"I didn't expect to see changes so quickly."* Were they inspecting him as they watched him from across the room, the way he wriggled his nose, maybe an extended jaw, tufts of hair on the tips of his ears?

Garik shivered in the growing silence.

Rapping on the door broke the moment, and they turned to see Nurse Leah peering inside.

"My goodness, girl," T'Wana let out, her body melting out of its formality for a moment before straightening. "You nearly took my breath away."

"My apologies, Tee. Dr. Jamie?" Leah smiled brightly. "You remember Justin. Michelle requests a few moments of your time. It seems Justin has been acting out again, and, um, well, Michelle seems to think this is pretty urgent."

"Michelle?" Garik frowned. He didn't like names being bandied about, like he was an experiment in a high school petri dish, and it didn't matter what they said around him, because they would throw him out as soon as he failed to produce the desired effect.

Jimenez groaned. "Leah, has she tried calling Justin by his name? That's all he wants, for her to remember his name and *use it,* for goodness' sake."

"I think she will listen to you better than to me." Leah smiled. "Can I tell her you are coming?"

"I'll be right there. Thank you, Leah. Now, Garik," and he released Garik's shoulders with a bright sound in his voice, "I'm leaving you with T'Wana and Van. They have some things to discuss with you. If you have any questions, feel free to ask. They know what they can share with you, and anything else, well, organize your questions, and I'll see you again, perhaps even later today. Okay?"

Garik shrugged. He was glad the man's arm was gone, but he also missed the small familiarity, even if he knew it was false. Through the window, if it was even a window, the image of his childhood home had touched a tender spot inside. His mama's hug, a pat on the head from his papa.

"Okay, then." Jimenez shifted his attention, moving on from Garik. "T'Wana, Van, you've got this until I can get free, right?"

"Certainly, Dr. Jamie," the two stumbled over themselves to say.

Jimenez disappeared out the door, kicking up the doorstop and letting the door click shut behind him. The sound of the latch clicking was a jailer's key to Garik's ears. When Van checked his pocket and pulled out a passkey, smiling and taking a breath of reassurance, it seemed to say that he was glad he wasn't locked in, and the truth washed over Garik like hot butter over a prepackaged waffle.

He was lunch. That's all there was to it, ready to be eaten up, regurgitated if he didn't go down well, and tossed out with the rubbish.

And no one would know, because no one knew he was here.

GARIK PULLED a shirt over his head, a plain gray tee with a flat, woven collar around the neck. T'Wana and Van had allowed him to select an outfit from the closet and dress, for which he was grateful. If he was going to sprout wolf fur from his back, he'd as soon have it covered as out for someone to observe, document, and record in a computer file somewhere that he would never be privy to.

Wolf boy in human clothing. Watch out, watch out! It might be his canines, next. Open wide. What big teeth you have, Garik, my boy!

He rolled his pajamas and tucked them under the sink. He didn't know how often he would receive fresh ones, and none of the doors in his room had revealed any laundry facilities, yet.

He studied his face in the mirror, wished for a cap, and remembered Marisa tying his hair into a bun for their visit with Ms. Sunchaser to tour Corona Tower. He blinked his eyes to clear them, then pressed the back of one hand to each side of his face, sniffling.

Marisa. He took a deep breath, lifted his right shoulder to his face and dried that eye, and then his left.

He shook his head in dismay when he saw two damp crescents on his shoulders. Okay, let them see. They needed to know what this was doing to him. He turned, pulled the door back and turned out the light.

"First," he demanded, determined that this time they would listen to him, "I have some questions."

T'Wana and Van were seated on the small couch, and they smiled and nodded. Van said, "We expected you would. Shoot, my friend."

"That's not a real window." Garik pointed to the obvious.

"Dr. Jamie was surprised you saw through that so quickly." Van smiled.

"Nothing to see through. That tree was struck by lightning when I was seven. Half of it was gone. It never grew back."

"Oh." Van and T'Wana glanced at each other with raised eyebrows. "You said questions. Next?"

"Who is Michelle?"

"You'll meet her later—"

"You'll tell me now." Garik crossed his arms. "I'm tired of being treated like I'm an experiment. Who's Michelle?"

"Michelle Vasquez." T'Wana stood, and she glanced from Van to Garik, obviously considering how much to say. "A nurse, like Leah—"

"Except not like Leah." That was plain to Garik. "Leah does medical things, like give me shots when I fight back. She was clear that Michelle wasn't doing that, so why isn't Michelle giving *Justin* a shot? Just knock him out? You people did me more than once, as everyone keeps telling me." He rubbed the stubble on the top of his head. "I don't even remember this growing, but I remember when it wasn't there at all. So, who's Michelle?"

Van stood this time, and he touched T'Wana's arm. "I'll take the blame for this. Garik, some of our research subjects need help adjusting, and not just with developing their skills. They need more." He grimaced and touched his temple. "Michelle is our . . ." he hesitated, then blurted out, "psychiatric nurse."

T'Wana made a face when Van said the words.

Crazy people, Garik thought, and dread flooded his brain with an explosive rush. What they do to people here makes them crazy.

And they'd already done it to him. Sheesh!

— 3 —

arik looked upward, his heart pounding. *This? They had a climbing wall?*

He was on his "orientation" with Van and T'Wana, and they had been joined by a short man with Cambodian eyes but an Irish complexion, crisply turned out in a military uniform and excessively polite.

"Do you like?" Senior Airman Shan Vang smiled at Garik, the perfect blend of manners and consideration for the young man's exposure to the new world of the Tower's basement research complex.

"What's not to like?" Garik had never used a climbing wall, so he wasn't entirely sure how they were supposed to be laid out. Arik, his aunt's boyfriend, liked to watch Wall Warriors, a competition series on television. Their climbing walls were nothing like this.

This one shot up through the floor above—Basement Level 1, if the sign on Garik's door meant anything—and the upper portion was filled on three sides with observation windows, where, Garik assumed, people on the upper floor could view the goings on up and down the climbing wall, including goof-ups, like his. He felt the hairs on his arms stand up just thinking about it. Higher were loops, straps, and harnesses hanging from ceiling gantries, several which appeared motorized. Half the wall had grips spaced impractically far apart.

"There, how could anyone climb that?" Garik nodded his head at the portion of the wall with the crazy distances between the grips.

"You've climbed, then?" Vang glanced at T'Wana and Van, slightly disapproving, without answering Garik's question. "I wasn't told."

"Are you kidding?" Garik laughed. Him? He was lucky Bay City had built the skate park. If they had built a climbing wall, he was certain he would have been on it—and broken an arm or leg or two. Besides, he didn't have to climb to see that no one's arms were that long. Unless someone could fly, well, and that was impossible. "I skate."

"Ah. That I knew." Vang's forehead smoothed, and Garik's two overseers began to breathe again. "Would you like to try?" He motioned to the wall.

"Can I?" Garik looked to Van. Dr. Jamie hadn't returned, and T'Wana seemed kind but afraid to decide without him. Van had told him about Michelle, and that had created a link, however tenuous, between the two. He didn't trust the Senior Airman, not that he distrusted him. He didn't *know* him.

"I'm sure Dr. Jamie would appreciate knowing if these are skills you might develop. Climbing, you understand. And I'm sure he will accede to my authority. I am, after all, your occupational therapist. We'll never know what occupation you can pursue if we never pursue one, will we? Besides, it's good exercise. Keeps you fit."

Van clapped Garik on the shoulder, hard enough to make him stumble. Garik frowned, but Van was smiling, not in an unfriendly way, and T'Wana nodded her agreement.

Vang gently touched Van's sleeve and said with an even, polite undertone, "Careful with the subject, Mr. Hermoso. We don't know his limits, yet."

Subject? Garik glanced at the Airman, ready to retort that he had a name. Vang was leaning in close to Van's ear, and T'Wana wore a pasted-on smile, waiting to see what was next on the "orientation" agenda, patently oblivious to the Airman's caution. Yet, Garik had heard him fine. Had he intended for him to hear? If so, why would he call him that? Maybe the man wasn't as kind as he seemed. Garik shivered.

Then he latched onto the rest of what the man had said. *We don't know his limits, yet.*

That was funny. He was seventeen, only recently a senior at Bay City High, and that was only if they ever let him out of this place. The unexpected reminder of his life outside his new prison—however fancy it might be—made him long for Ibn, Muhammad, even the three shrimps, Winter, Firestarter, and Shrimper. Especially Robbie, who was like a little brother. Garik had stayed over his place like a second home on nights when his aunt worked late before she went on assistance.

"Can we do this?" Garik drew in a deep breath, hiding his emotions behind a wall of action. He pointed upward. "Do I need one of those?"

"A harness, yes." Vang smiled. "Mr. Hermoso, we should give the boy a chance to experience some of what we have to offer. This will be a good test of his progress. Ms. Dolalas? Is our young man ready?"

"I suppose so, though I haven't personally evaluated him. Dr. Jamie only introduced us this morning, and then he was called away."

"Yes, with Justin. We are all aware. Still, you are unaware of any reason we shouldn't proceed? He will be in a harness and unlikely to fall."

"I don't fall." Garik said the words hard, angry

bravado overriding his sense of caution. He was deciding he didn't like this Airman as much as the one he already knew. He would show him.

"I am pleased to hear that." Vang tapped his watch, and Garik noticed a flesh-toned earbud in his ear. "I need Maye here. We require the climbing wall." After a moment, he said, "We're here now. So, stat."

The Airman looked up, pleased. He motioned to Garik, walked with him to the wall and grasped a plastic protrusion bolted to the undulating surface.

"This is us." He wrenched the grip in several ways, and it failed to budge. "You are you. We remain the same." He rapped the grip with his knuckles, a hollow plastic sound, for emphasis. "You must adapt to us. It is easy. We provide the structure; you learn to make your way forward. Do you have questions?"

Structure? Adapt? Garik wanted to laugh. He also wanted to climb this wall, and that wouldn't happen if he offended this man.

"Can we do this now?" That would have to do—for the moment.

"Certainly. I see Mr. Maye arriving. I will put you in his capable hands. I'm looking forward to this demonstration, and I'm sure you will perform admirably."

Vang stepped back, and Garik turned to see a tall, fit, blond man striding his direction with a broad smile. Nordic in skin tone and facial structure, he carried a climbing harness with a waist belt, two leg loops, and several metal eyes to attach gear and the safety lines hanging from the ceiling.

"Garik!" The man raised one hand is an open-palm wave, his five digits like a gleaming star, as if they were old friends. "I hope you like first names. I'm Devon, the recreation coordinator and activities director around here. I've been hearing good things about you."

"Sure." *Hearing good things about me?* Garik had no idea what that meant. "You are going to help me climb this?"

"Right-o, kiddo." Devon grinned. "Let's see how well I chose your harness."

Devon knelt, held the harness to Garik's waist, and checked each of the leg loops. He adjusted the buckle on the waist belt, shortened the leg loops slightly, and stood with a grin.

"I need to put that on?" Garik glanced to Van for confirmation, to see him nod.

"Devon knows what he's doing. I'm here to observe how you perform, but Devon's in charge of this. Just do what he says."

"Okay. Do I keep my shoes on or off?"

"Ack!" Devon hit his forehead with one hand, causing Garik to notice a pronounced cowlick at his left temple. He laughed, not at all irritated. "Shoes, shoes! No one tells me they need shoes."

"I'm sorry," Garik said, apologizing for something

that wasn't his fault but that he felt was his responsibility, somehow.

"Here." Devon grinned expectantly as he unzipped the largest fanny pack in the world. "I might have an extra pair in here." He pulled out a pair of thin, rubberized shoes, with a wide, Velcro flap to hold them on.

Garik turned at a hand on his shoulder to see Van at his side. Van said, "See? Devon has you covered."

The touch of the hand, the magic pair of shoes, and the climbing wall at his side . . . Garik's frustration and anger softened a bit, and in that moment, he felt a surge of anticipation.

I can do this. I know I can.

He looked up at the wall, excited, and he was certain he would reach the top and be better than anyone ever had before.

Just watch, Airman Vang. I'll show you.

GARIK GASPED as he hit the bottom of the safety line's arc. He had fallen five times already, and his legs were sure to bleed bruises before morning.

"I'm all right," he called to those below him. Devon held the end of the safety line where it looped up through a pulley attached to a ceiling gantry and anchored to Garik's harness on the other.

"We'll move you over and try again," Devon called. "Hold steady while I shift your position."

A machine attached to the pulley began to whine,

Garik felt the carabiners at his waist shift and jerk, and the wall moved closer. Vang had abandoned the demonstration, except for cursory attention from time to time. The man normally lifted his head and spoke down his nose, and he wasn't doing that now, which meant the man wasn't interacting with or showing interest in Garik's current progress.

What was Garik saying? *He* wasn't interested in his current progress, because he wasn't making any.

Van still called out encouragements.

"Swell job," and, "Way to go, Garik." Garik knew better. Swell meant you didn't fall six times, and with everyone watching, too.

Dr. Jimenez had joined them about the third fall, cutting Garik's humiliation even deeper and adding raw sandpaper to the mix. And the things they'd been saying to one another. "The Director will be disappointed." "He should be making progress by now." "Even Marco could do the climbing wall after only three weeks."

Three weeks? This was Garik's first day, at least the first day he was off the "sleepy juice." He'd show Marco in another three weeks.

Then someone, Van, Garik thought, said, "Marco? Marco Lopez? Whoa, I didn't know that."

Devon said, plenty loud for Garik to hear, "Yes, and he's a confirmed failure."

Garik had no idea who Marco was, except a confirmed failure, but now he knew he was worse than

Marco. What was less than a failure? A slug? A blight on the research program's record? One of the "things" on the Basement 5 level?

Is that what would happen to him? His body would degenerate into something soft and unrecognizable? He'd already lost muscle tone. The mirror that morning had proved that. Would he even recognize himself in the morning?

He looked up, the glass and hard surfaces surrounding him causing the conversations below to reverberate in his ears. He heard Vang, and he glanced down to see him at the doctor's side, his mouth covered like that made it alright to talk so loudly.

"This is not what I hoped to see. I trust we don't need to write off another of your subjects."

"I still feel hopeful," Jimenez replied. "The Director's transformation spanned six months, and much of that was touch and go. Look at him now."

"Agreed. This one? He's too soft—"

"I can hear you," Garik yelled down the shaft to the floor below.

They looked up. Jimenez smiled. "Then there's that."

"Yes, there's that." Vang dropped his hand, lifted his nose, and said the words grudgingly. "If it's anything."

Garik shook his head in dismay.

"Use the red grips this time," Devon called, his

voice light and positive. "We'll try a different route."

Garik, hanging from the ceiling, the straps on his legs making them into segmented sausage links, looked at his hands. The grips smelled . . . like people. Who, he didn't know, but he had identified sixteen different people who had climbed the wall since it was last sanitized. Or maybe it was never sanitized. Who cared if confirmed failures transmitted viruses or other germs via the grips on the wall?

He knew one thing: Devon had climbed the wall, and he was good. Devon had helped attach his harness, tightening it around his waist, then giving him instructions on how to tighten the leg straps. At one point, he'd taken Garik's hand and shown him how to place his fingers and grip the plastic protrusions on the wall. The aroma left on his skin was clean and fresh, a whiff of spruce and flowing mountain streams. His smell was all over the blue and nowhere else, meaning he was better than good, but not even Devon seemed to have made it to the part with the impossible grips.

Garik began making his way along the red route, stretching, suspecting that only *tall* people could do some of the routes, and that wasn't him. He caught more odors, individual smells that were as distinct as the fingerprints on people's hands, but not any he was familiar with. What did that mean? When one hand slipped off the same grip twice, he gasped, thinking, *C'mon, people. I know how tall I am. Can't you tell?*

Give me something I can do.

In a last effort to prove himself, he stretched and leaped for one of the "impossible" handholds. They were there for some reason. They couldn't be just decoration. Maybe this was the way. He touched it, felt it slide through his fingers, and he was airborne, in freefall for what seemed forever, then the safety line caught him, jerking hard against his waist and legs, and he hung, limp, sweaty, and exhausted.

Devon caught him, let out a poorly disguised, "Oomph," then muttered, "Man, even Amy could do the red route."

Garik felt his eyes water, and he didn't want tears. He squashed them shut. Even *Amy* was better than he was, and he didn't even know who Amy was. Frustration and self-loathing seeped from under his eyelids. Devon was disappointed in him, Vang said he was too soft, and Van. Even Van had stopped calling out his bright if banal encouragements.

Leave me here, he thought. I can't come down and face you people.

But he wasn't so depressed that he couldn't hear Vang say, "I can't see anything positive in this subject."

"I can still hear you!"

Were they *trying* to make him more miserable than he already was? Good luck with that!

— 4 —

G

arik stripped away the climbing gear, a volcanic level of shame and embarrassment at his abject failure forcing his eyes to the floor, where they caught nothing but feet, feet, and more feet, all of people who had found their niche in whatever program he had been sucked into in the dank bowels of the Corona Tower basement.

Deported. He was here, wasn't he?

Marisa had been lied to, and *there was nothing he could do about it!* He couldn't even climb the wall that *Amy* could do. What was he going to do, shout at them, force them into letting him go? *They* had the needle.

They had Nurse Ratchett. *They* had all the power, and he had none at all.

Garik held the climbing harness, the magic that he had so recently strapped to his legs while his heart had raced with excitement. He fumbled with resetting the buckles, unable to get them to readjust to their original settings. He was going to show Airman Vang. He was going to be the best, maybe even be a success at the part of the wall that was impossible to climb. Now, his throat was a knotted rope, and it squeezed moisture from his eyes.

He wadded the harness in one fist and knelt to remove Devon's shoes, forcing his shoulders to his face, pressing one to each eye, and he tried to stifle a ragged breath as he involuntarily sucked air down his windpipe and into his burning chest. He remembered the damp crescents from that morning. They would know. They *would know* he had been forced to tears. It was yet another mortification on top of every other failure that had bitten into his day and spat him back out, ragged and exposed for everyone to see.

A hand clasped him on the shoulder, and an open palm interrupted his misery. "Harness?" Four fingers flexed, reminding Garik of Arik when he wanted to confiscate something that didn't belong to him.

"Harness," Garik repeated and felt a tear run down one cheek, once more mortified. Just the one word had revealed his ragged emotions. His chest shook as another stumbling breath fought its way down his throat.

"Hey." Devon's face appeared at his side as the tall, blond man knelt beside him, leaning in and speaking in a whisper. His hand found the back of Garik's neck. "It's okay, kiddo. It's your first time on the wall."

"Amy could do it." Garik felt his nose turn loose, and he brushed it with the back of his wrist. He refused to look at the man.

"You heard that." Devon sat up and blew out a hard breath.

"Yeah, and Marco, and the Director will be disappointed. And Airman Vang wants to write me off." Repeating it made him angry. "Is that what you think? And Van, he thinks I'm a disappointment, too?"

Devon leaned back in, his hand still on Garik's neck. "No one thinks you're a disappointment."

"Van quit encouraging me, and now they're all over there, probably deciding to kick me out the door."

"You're not lucky enough for that, I'll promise you now." Devon chuckled, and he squeezed Garik's neck before patting him on the back. "C'mon, while they aren't looking, and we'll get you somewhere you can clean up. No sense in being more embarrassed than you already are."

"Okay." Garik glanced over to see Airman Vang looking down his nose and saying something to Dr. Jimenez. Neat, polite, but not nice. Garik frowned.

"What?" Devon stood, and he looked that direction.

"Terminate. What does Airman Vang want to terminate?"

"You can hear that?" Devon wrapped his fingers around Garik's arm and pulled him to his feet. He called to the others, "Showers! I won't let him wander off."

Devon waited until Jimenez looked their direction and held up a hand in recognition before he dropped his arm. The good doctor was making an animated point with the calm, ever-polite Vang.

"So, what was the doctor saying back there?" Devon took Garik's harness and the shoes. He tucked them into his fanny pack and held out Garik's shoes. "You can carry these."

"What do you mean?" Garik tucked the shoes under his arm. Devon had started moving, and he matched his pace.

"Just curious. I want your opinion."

"You, first." Garik was warming to the man, and he wasn't sure he liked the feeling. No one here, *no one*, meant good to him. They were all part of locking him away without his permission and lying to everyone about where he was. Every one of them.

"Right-o, kiddo." Devon laughed as if this were an inside joke, one they had shared before. "I think they were saying they were wrong, and they expect you to exceed on every test they give you, put you at the top of every leaderboard in the facility."

"Right. As if." Garik caught Devon's wink, the blond cowlick making him boyish and approachable, like Devon enjoyed a good time more than he enjoyed the people who were over him in this place.

"Your turn. Spill." Devon grinned. "Give up the goods on the good doctor."

"He told Vang I'm double fortunate to be in the program, and he would terminate me only when I proved I was a failure."

"Ouch." Devon stopped, causing Garik to almost run into him. They had reached what served as the locker room for the climbing wall, and Devon paused before opening the door. "I'm sorry you heard that. Hey, look, I don't tell everyone this, but my mother died of ALS. Do you know what that is?"

"That baseball player's disease?"

"Yes. It causes your muscles to waste away. And I'll tell you this, my mother was no failure. Forget them. You come back to the wall anytime. You'll get it eventually."

"You'll teach me? You're good. You've done every blue route. I could tell." Garik grinned. "Just none of the impossible ones."

"How could you tell that?" Devon frowned.

"Your smell. It's trees and water." *None of the impossible ones.* Would he never learn? Garik pleaded with his eyes for Devon to forgive him.

"I—" Devon smelled of his hand. "I don't—" He shook his head. "And you heard the doctor back there."

"You did, too," Garik said. "You must."

"Have they told you what they, um—" He paused and looked around. "—what they *mixed* you with?"

"Oh, timber wolf."

Devon shook his head and closed his eyes, and when he opened them, he smiled.

"What?" Garik felt his frustration building. *Just say it!*

"Timber wolf. That explains a lot. I'll need to watch what I say *and* the soap I use."

"What does that mean?"

"Nothing, kiddo. Wolf is good, better than what Hefferly got. I might even like you if you stick around. So, stick around. Now, inside and get cleaned up. Here, I even have a change of clothes for you." He dug in his pack and pulled out a tee, pants, and underwear, all in Garik's size.

"Mine are clean." Garik accepted the clothes grudgingly only when Devon forced them on him.

"Not after that in there. Go all the way through. The shower room is in the back. Soap and towels are inside. I'll wait here. Make it quick. *They* want you back again, and we don't want them to wait too long. Right-o, kiddo?"

"Right-o," and Garik slipped inside the door and let it close behind him.

WHAT HEFFERLY got. The words churned in Garik's mind, leaving red-hot embers in their wake.

What did Devon mean? Garik had grabbed Hefferly's arm, twisted, and the man's arm had evaporated in his grasp.

Hadn't it? Or had it only seemed that way?

Then, there was Amy, an unqualified success at the red route. Was she a "subject" also? Or Marco. He was a failure, and he had been a success on the climbing wall.

And why would Devon need to watch what he said around him? Or his soap? Garik was just Garik, with no differences, none except what these people had done to him.

He dried his face and, with the towel, cleared a small circle in the mirror. He studied his eyebrows, his nose, and his chin. He could hardly forgive them for his hair, but that was something *they* had done, perhaps to disguise his appearance. Who knew? The rest of him? Softer was from lack of exercise, that was all. With Van's help, and now that Devon was offering him extra time on the climbing wall—

Still, through everything, Vang's words kept toying with his mind. *"The Director will be disappointed."* And, *"I trust we don't need to write off another of your subjects."*

Him. He was talking about *him*. Garik.

He pictured himself in one of the cages on the Basement 5 level, the sad eyes looking at him and Marisa, the grasping hands, and the hopelessness they'd seen there.

Marisa! He wanted to protect her as never before, and he couldn't, not locked in here. They had lied to her, threatened her family, said they would destroy her family's business if she said anything about the Tower's basements and what they had found inside. It wasn't fair!

He couldn't bear to see himself in the mirror— helpless and soft and weak—and he wadded the towel and forced it to the glass, pressed hard, trying to make himself disappear into the steam and fog in the shower room.

Rage crawled out of him in a scream as he began to pound the glass. He wasn't sure if it was his voice or the glass breaking, but before he exhausted his fury, warmth flowed down his arm, and sirens wailed around him. Devon burst into the room, groaned and said, "I'm in trouble now," and he reached into his pack, pulled out a syringe, and plunged it into Garik's arm.

Garik wasn't sure if things were better after that or if he just didn't care. He looked into Devon's face, thought he saw his lips say, "I'm sorry," and the alarm and lights faded away.

THIS TIME when Garik woke, he recognized the light.

Not Heaven. He waited for it to morph into the familiar light fixture before looking around.

The machines. The clinic. He heard a sound behind him. "Am I getting another injection?"

"Why would you ask that?" A pretty voice, with a familiar undertone.

"Needles, needles, needles. Anything that happens, you people poke me with a needle. What was it this time?"

"You don't remember?"

The unfamiliar voice moved into view, and for Garik, the room narrowed with shock. He tried to sit up, only to be gently pressed back to the bed.

"Not okay. You're not badly hurt, but you are hurt."

"I'm not strapped down?" He looked at his feet. His ankles were bare, but no straps. His wrists, none there, either.

"Not if you behave, and I suggest you behave." She took his arm and held it to where he could see the bandages. "I don't know how many stitches, but many. Now, lie still. Head back. Less talking."

"I know you." Big eyes. Black hair. Below her chin, though, things weren't so normal. Scales on her neck, flaps that were perhaps gill openings, bigger on her right side, and webs between her fingers on her right hand. He noticed she continually kept her left side turned his direction, as if the changes bothered her. "You're Marina."

"Yes." She smiled.

"Your mother was right. Marisa looks a lot like you." Garik watched her face, seeing Marisa in her sister, and suddenly more heartsick than he had been yet.

"You'll make me cry." Marina looked away, and she patted her face with her fingers, finally wiping her cheeks. "I know of you, that you were captured to allow Marisa to escape. Thank you."

"Okay." He hadn't thought of it that way at the time, but it made him feel a little better that she had escaped because of him, even if he'd rather that he'd escaped with her.

"You don't seem surprised to see me." Marina smiled, clearly teasing him, so much like her sister.

"Mr. Choi thought Marisa was you, and when I saw you, I immediately understood."

"That's the wolf in you."

"Aargh! Does everyone know?" Garik threw his head back and slammed his fists down on the bed. His right hand began to throb.

"I suggested you behave." Marina patted his throbbing arm. "I really liked Mr. Choi. Thank you for telling me that he remembers. Now, we can head you back to your room. B2-17, right?"

"You even know that. Don't I get any secrets?"

"I sincerely hope so. Here's one you can appreciate. Wolf is very good, better than what they've tried on some of us. Enjoy your differences. If you see Marisa again—" She took a deep breath, smiled, and said, "Never mind. Stand up. Let's get you to your room. It's two floors up. I'll be going with you, just to see that you arrive, okay?"

"My jailer."

"Your friend, if you want me to be."

He grinned. "Any friend of Marisa's—"

"—is welcome to be a friend of mine." She pulled out a passkey, slipped it into the door mechanism, and when the metal deadbolts thumped noisily, she removed it and opened the door. "With me, please."

Garik did look at his arms as they passed the climbing wall on the way back to his room. Two hands, one wolf and the other human. Is that how his life would play out? Is that why Marina was hidden away? Clearly, she was fully functional.

He didn't want to be locked away in the basements of Corona Tower for the rest of his life. Surely there was a way out.

He just had to find it.

— 5 —

arina, do I have to go back inside now?"

The sight of his door—B2-17—made Garik's skin crawl. It might be filled with everything a body needed to live, including furniture, good electronics—if he ever got the chance to use them—and a closet filled with clothes, but it also had a lock on the door, one that he didn't have a key to.

A prison was a prison was a prison, no matter how they styled it up to look like a place someone might want to live.

She had her passkey out, Garik noticed. It was

required from the outside as well as the inside. He couldn't get out, but by the same measure, no one could get in, not unless they had the magic stick.

What did that mean? What would they want to keep out of his room that might want to get in?

He was no longer thinking *who* might want to get in. He had seen too much. DNA. Timber wolf. Marina in her fish clothing. Jantzen Hefferly's effervescent wrist, evaporating into smoke at the touch of Garik's hand.

It was no longer *who* might want to get in his room but *what*. Garik's thoughts had shifted as easily from one concept to the other as a man might slip down a greased pole from one level of a firehouse to another, disappearing into the dark hole in the floor to face whatever awaits him, good or bad.

"Where have you been allowed to visit so far?" Marina paused, wrapped her passkey in her hand and, after a moment, turned toward Garik.

Her eyes, a slight shifting of her lips, the anticipation of his answer. Garik remembered that night on the roof with Marisa. They each had wrapped up in blankets against the cold dark, and the sound of the Dactyls had filtered through the night air. Marisa was focused on her MicroArt tablet, furiously scribbling away on her latest graphic storyboard, and she had handed it to him to see—

"The electrified sword. I haven't seen that." He said

it with an assurance he didn't know he possessed. It was thinking of Marisa. She had been captivated by the idea of the sword, even giving him a drawing of her wearing two of them when she knew Arik was coming down on him. Well, was about to come down on him, but it was the same. She had offered him protection from what she knew was coming, even if it was only ink on paper. He wanted to reach out to her and protect her now, and he couldn't.

Still, the sword was a connection to her. If he could see it, know where it was, even—though he couldn't imagine this would happen—touch it, hold it, wield it to fight his way out of this place—

"I was told you were a bit of a dreamer." Marina touched his arm. Garik jerked back to the corridor, startled to see the ordinary lights overhead, his door, B2-17, beside him, and Marina looking at him with a smile that reminded him of her sister.

"Dreamer. What do you mean?" His heart wasn't yet settled from his conquest of his dungeon prison, and he realized he could identify Marina's fragrance. "You are seaweed and the beach, did you know that?"

"What?" She laughed, pretty in the moment, and clear and guileless in her surprise. "Where did that come from?"

"I don't know." Garik shrugged. "You just are. It smells good, you know, the shore. Marisa and I used to walk to The Docks—"

"Don't tell me I smell like The Docks." Marina chuckled, her left hand at her mouth to quiet the sound. "I've lived in Bay City all my life, and that place is diesel and death. Yuck."

"No, wait." Garik would be irritated at himself for his clumsiness, but Marina seemed not to mind. He grinned. "Not The Docks. We would walk down Shorefront to Cassel Dunes and watch the surf come in. The wind would come in from the water, always cold, and the smell was like the world was brand new, and we were the only people in it."

"Seaweed, though?"

"Seaweed's not a bad thing." Garik shrugged again, though not as big as before. "It's just part of it. I like seaweed."

"Okay, then. I just never thought I smelled like seaweed." She lifted the inside of her wrist to her nose and drew in a dramatically deep breath before moving her arm away.

"And the beach," Garik reminded her.

"And the beach, so that makes seaweed okay. I can live with that." She glanced down the corridor both ways, as if deciding what she might be permitted to show him. Her eyes settled on the large room Garik had seen earlier from through his door. "Follow me. I don't think I can give you the sword, but I can show you a few other things. You must promise to behave."

"I promise." He lifted his arm to pledge his cooperation, saw the bandages, and changed arms. "I don't guess my bandages are much reassurance."

"Your promise is enough. Just be good." She waggled a finger at him before turning to lead him through the opening into the vast space beyond. "I'll need to pick up a tablet. I can get one in the clinic."

MUCH OF Basement Level 2 was off limits to Garik, he quickly found. Marina showed him the small clinic first, where she put in a code and withdrew a tablet and a stylus from a cabinet and signed in.

"What's that for?"

"I have to let them know you're with me. Have they told you about the heat sensors?"

"Yeah. They supposedly don't spy on me, but they do. What about them?"

"Don't be too harsh with them. They might save your life. It's not my place to say too much, and I'm not an expert on what will happen to you in the next few months, but you will change. Anyway, this way they will know why you aren't in your room."

No one was inside the clinic, so they only glanced around. Marina left the lights off, as they had found them. "The clinic is only for emergencies," she said, and Garik pictured his bandaged arm, wondering what constituted an emergency.

He did notice that Marina signed out a small container of lotion, and as they continued, she opened it and began working it into the skin on her right arm. She didn't explain, and pretty soon, Garik's mind had turned to other things.

The climbing wall was only one part of a much larger recreation area, with running tracks, boxing rings, and gymnastic equipment. One wall of glass fronted a water-filled room.

"That's recreation?" Garik walked to the wall, looking into the blue-tiled cavern, seeing resting places and tables underwater. It didn't look like the pool in the upper floors of the Tower that he had visited with Marisa and Kevin Lee. "Who uses that?"

"Me."

Garik turned, mortified at his continued clumsiness. "Oh. I didn't think. I'm sorry. I forget—" He cut off his words before he said something else he would regret.

"Don't apologize. I'm glad you see me and not what I've become. Let's move on."

They were walking past a long set of interior windows, plain glass backed with blinds, when Garik asked, "Why did you call me a dreamer?"

"That?" She laughed lightly. "I'm sorry. I should have watched my words. It's nothing."

"Marisa calls me a dreamer." He felt his eyes tighten with memories and shook them off. "So, why am I a dreamer, and who's been telling you that?"

"It's the way you pause, lost in your own world, and you have to be reminded that someone's talking to you—"

A loud, unexpected voice interrupted her. "There you are! Marina, wait!"

"Caught out." Marina wrapped her hand around Garik's good wrist and whispered as she laughed. "This is likely the end of our tour. It's Jantzen."

"Hefferly?" Garik knew who she meant. He just didn't know if they would meet the man from the video screens in the food court, the man who had seemed compassionate in the hospital room, or the one who had jerked away in pain when Garik had grabbed his wrist. He felt his body tense in anticipation.

"You promised." Marina gave his wrist another squeeze before releasing it.

"Be good. Right." Garik tried to relax, but the memory of the needles wasn't a good one, and to him, even though the man had seemed to have kind eyes, he also hadn't hung around to stand up for him when Dr. Jimenez had instructed Nurse Ratchett to shove the needle back in his arm to send him off to sleepy land.

"Thank you." She turned, lifted her left hand to her hair, pushed it through, and let it fall back in exactly the same place as before. "Jantzen, hello. What can I do for you? I'm taking Garik on a walkabout—"

"I know. Thank you." Jantzen stopped at their side with a smile. He straightened his dark-gray shirt with its long sleeves and shook one leg to line up a crease to center on a gleaming leather oxford. As he brushed the front of his pants flat, the black face of his watch peeked from inside his sleeve before disappearing once more. He looked almost ordinary, but his dark hair and tight beard did nothing to disguise the glint of purple from his dark eyes. "I would like to borrow Mr. Shayk for a time."

"Garik." The word was out before Garik took time to think.

"I remember. My apologies, Garik. I wasn't sure if Marina . . ." He looked at her and back to Garik. "You are familiar with one another?"

"Yes," Marina replied, leaving it at that.

"Then, Garik, you will understand that Marina needs to hydrate. I was surprised to see her leading your tour. Marina?" He smiled at her, nodded his head, and clearly dismissed her.

"Of course. Enjoy the rest of your tour, Garik." She smiled and stepped back. As she walked away, she pulled out her tablet and marked on it, holding it very much as Marisa had held her MicroArt tablet that night on the roof.

"Let's visit the break area. Meals are always taken on the floor above, but we don't want you to starve." Jantzen was ebullient, as if wishing to put his best foot forward. "This way. Very well stocked, even if I prefer regular meals over snacking."

"If my door's always locked—"

"I know." Jantzen grimaced. "But, you understand,

this is a research facility, and for now, you're an unknown. But you have T'Wana and Van assigned to you—"

"Assigned to me?"

"Of course." The corridor opened up on one side to a large space with tables, chairs, and lounging spaces, a large screen on the wall, and a kitchen area and refrigerator hunkering in one corner.

"To only me?" As what, monitors, overseers, or even guards?

"Yes." Jantzen's answer was blunt, and he let his word hang without elaborating. He pulled two canned drinks from the fridge and motioned to a table. He handed one drink to Garik before pulling the tab on his. Once Garik was seated, Jantzen pulled out a chair and seated himself casually.

"Okay?" Garik could wait. Answers were what he wanted.

Jantzen let out a sigh, licked his lips, and took a sip of his drink. He leaned forward and placed both arms on the table, as if about to reveal something important. "This can't be easy for you—"

"Yah!" The word burst from Garik. "You figured that out? It took you this long? Sheesh! Stupidity fills every corridor in this place."

"Okay. I deserved that. *We* deserved that." Jantzen leaned back, took in a deep breath, and grinned sheepishly. He tapped the table for a moment with his fingers before saying, "I am sorry—"

"Just not enough to let me go." Garik's words came out like a fist into a punching bag.

"Some things I can't control. Some things I can. I can take you on a more exhaustive tour than Marina could. Does that interest you?"

"Maybe. Tell me this, first. You know Marina. Upstairs, Ms. Sunchaser acted like she never heard of her. Is everything here lies?"

"They're wrong about you." Jantzen studied Garik out of his purple eyes.

"How?"

"You're not a failure. I can already see you are becoming exactly what you are meant to be."

"I'm meant to be seventeen. I'm meant to be a senior at Bay City High next year. I'm meant to be me, Garik, not some monster you lock in a cage." By then, Garik was furious, and he pictured the cages on Basement Level 5, but he couldn't say that. It might make it true, and that was too much to stomach right then.

"How about that tour?" Jantzen stood, leaving his unfinished drink on the table. "Maybe some time to cool down will be good for us."

"Hmph." Garik refused to reply.

Jantzen looked at him, and as he stepped back to push in his chair, he murmured, "Maybe more than they intend him to be."

"I heard that," Garik said, trying to decide if he

should like this man or not.

Jantzen paused a moment, as though to soak in something he hadn't expected. Finally, he grinned. "As I said, my young friend, no way are you a failure. You might be the best one yet. Follow me. I've got some things to show you."

Garik joined the slim, well-tailored man with his tight beard and dark looks, and they stepped out of the break area. The man had clearly whispered his remark, but not quietly enough. Had he intended for Garik to hear? Whatever, he had heard him fine. There, Mr. Hefferly. My secret's out. I heard every word you said, whether you wanted me to or not.

It didn't make Garik feel much better, but it was better than nothing, so he guessed it would have to do.

— 6 —

J

antzen Hefferly's first stop was at a door flanked by long walls of plate glass. The door boasted the tag, B2-Facilities Mgt. He leaned into the doorknob, faced Garik, and shrugged. "Even I have to report in." He winked and grinned before opening the door and pushing partially through. "Rachel, I've got the new kid with me. Code him in so we don't get any alarms."

Garik flicked his eyes down the identical windows with the same identical blinds—all closed—filling the corridor. He couldn't see who Jantzen was talking with, but he could hear her fine.

"I've got it already in the works. Marina had tentatively shifted him to you at the, um, yes, it's right here, at the break area. He's been with you since?" Rachel sounded very bright and efficient.

"Yes. If Weston asks, I need to acquaint myself with him, and—" his voice dropped in volume, but not too low for Garik to clearly understand, "—we had an incident earlier. I want to resolve this so Devon, well, it wasn't Devon's fault, and he doesn't deserve the reprimand I suspect is coming."

"Certainly." Garik heard the rapid staccato of a keyboard's rhythmic music. "There. That should give you as much time as you need."

"Thank you, Rachel." Jantzen pulled out of the doorway, and without any intervention, the door began to close, giving off the heavy metallic thump, thump of every door in the place when it closed and locked.

Garik had loved the sound when locking up his Street Strider. It was the sweet music of safety and security, of, "I'll still be here in the morning," but this was completely different. This metallic thump, thump now sang of abandonment and anger and the tedious existence of people who were no longer free.

"My apologies for excluding you, there." Jantzen nodded his head down the corridor, and he started forward, slower at first to let Garik catch up. "A little private time to handle a little necessary business. Now we can take the time we need to explore. How is your hand doing?"

"Okay." His conversation hadn't been exactly private. Garik had heard every word, but Jantzen's comment suggested he hadn't been meant to. He wondered why Devon would be in trouble. Sheesh. Nothing made sense down here.

"If that arm starts to bother you, let me know. You should heal pretty quickly, but you've just stepped on the first rung of the ladder. I don't know what changes are accelerating initially and which will take a while. It's been a few days since I've scanned your file. Devon said you mentioned Amy, and Dr. Jamie said Justin came up in conversation this morning."

"If you like." Jantzen moved quickly, and Garik was working to keep up. "Can you slow down? I haven't eaten lunch, and this is pretty quick."

"I forgot. Your first real day up and about. I'm guessing that's part of the reason for the disaster at the climbing wall." Jantzen cocked his head sideways and cut his eyes Garik's direction, his words a hot poker as though he wanted to see if any sparks flew.

"Maybe." Garik shrugged as if it didn't matter, and he attempted to thrust his hands in his pockets. One went in fine, and the other jammed on the bandages. Flustered, and embarrassed, he curled his bandaged hand at his chest and held the arm with his good one.

"Something else, then?" They had slowed, but now they approached an elevator, and Jantzen stopped and withdrew his passkey.

"Is that taking us to food?" Garik asked a real question, and he hoped he got a real answer. He *was* hungry, and he didn't know if he could find the break area, but he'd be glad to try. That required freedom, though, and Rachel had assigned Jantzen as his jailer.

"Certainly. The cafeteria up on One. You'll be expected to eat there once we feel you can wander the facility without supervision." Jantzen slipped in the passkey, the elevator came to life, and he withdrew the key. "After you," he motioned, when the doors opened.

Without supervision. Garik almost laughed. If you mean when I won't try to escape, that'll be never. Still, he was hungry, and he moved into the sumptuously quiet elevator, with its freshly deodorized and purified air. The panel by the door illuminated when he entered. It was so close. He wanted to reach out and touch it, tell it to take him to the lobby, but this didn't look like the one he had been in that fateful day when Marisa had taken them from the real world above into this warren of rooms and corridors that had trapped him in its spiderweb of lies. It was likely a basement-only elevator. They weren't apt to let him near one that might lead up into the light of possible escape or recognition by anyone he had known before.

His mind leaped to his hair and to school. He glanced up for the mirror that had been on the ceiling of the elevator that day only to see recessed panels of wood. With the current length of his hair, Bay City High was likely back in session. He wondered if his friends missed him, or if they had made new friends and he would soon be forgotten.

A familiar voice brought him back to the moment.

"Thank you, Dr. Hefferly, for holding the door. Up or down?"

"The cafeteria, so up. You?" Jantzen sounded courteous and patient, as if he knew the man approaching, and he was happy to share his elevator.

Garik wasn't so happy. He recognized the voice and involuntarily pressed his shoulder to the wall. It was Airman Vang, and he didn't want to be in this elevator car with him, not now, not tomorrow, not ever.

And there was nothing he could do. It was about to happen whether he wanted it to or not.

AIRMAN VANG stepped through the door, hesitated a fraction of a moment at the unexpected companion riding along, and nodded before turning to face the door. He was followed by a tightly built man with thinning hair and delicate features. His arms looked like they could bust bricks. Jantzen made the introductions as he inserted his passkey and pushed the button for Basement 1.

"Airman, I believe you've met our newest young man. Second Lt. Wilder, meet Garik Shayk, a recent participant in our studies."

"Shayk." Wilder nodded, acknowledging Garik. He glanced at the bandaged arm before turning to the front to stand by Airman Vang as the doors silently sealed them in.

"That's the one that went off on himself?" Wilder.

"Yes, but the runt has ears like a bat. Can hear you across the room." Vang, subvocalizing, but perfectly clear to Garik.

"Didn't know they were using bats. Thought that was too much of a Dracula thing." Wilder visibly shivered.

"Timber wolf. They hear almost as well."

"So, no Dracula, but werewolf is fine. Whatever floats their boats. Mongrels, each and every one." Wilder chuckled.

"Got that right," Vang replied.

The door opened, and the two stepped out without acknowledging the two people standing behind them. Garik shook his head in amazement. Vang should look in a mirror. That's where he would find a mongrel, as if he would even know what one was.

"Garik?" Jantzen stepped forward and turned when Garik didn't move.

"Why didn't you say something?" Garik wanted to smash the wall, but he had tried that, and now look at his arm.

"Okay." Jantzen frowned. "I introduced you. Lt. Wilder's first name is Ron. I was assured you knew

Airman Vang."

"No. What they said about me. Why did you let them say that? I'm a person, not a mongrel, a werewolf thing. Why didn't you tell them to shut up?" Garik felt his world tightening, his focus narrowing, the heat of his anger rising in his face.

"You heard all that?"

"I'm not a liar. You're telling me they didn't say it?"

"No, I'm telling you I didn't hear it. What else did they say?"

"That you don't use bats because it would make people think of Dracula." Not exactly, but that's what they meant.

"Okay, that's a near quote. Your hearing's better than I thought. I wouldn't share that ability with just anyone." Jantzen placed a finger to his lips and smiled.

"But why would they say that with me right here?"

"Because they thought you couldn't hear them. That's a pretty good trick you have, so don't give it away. Am I making myself clear?"

"Like your arm?" Garik started to put his hands in his pockets again, looked down at his bandaged one, and didn't know what to do with them.

"I didn't hide that very well, did I?" Jantzen laughed. "You'll feel better with food. I'm serious about how well you hear. No sense in giving away all the good stuff."

"Sure." Garik touched his lips and zipped them. "Can I get nachos?"

"Sure. And if they don't have them here, I can order from Chow Down. See? We get everything down here."

"Except a passkey." Garik whispered it, looked at Jantzen, and was convinced he didn't hear. He was learning. They were teaching him, and like he had said once before, if he ever got in the Tower, he could Houdini himself out.

Give him time, and he'd be gone.

GARIK DIDN'T get nachos. He learned the cafeteria wasn't always open, and he didn't want to wait on Chow Down, so Jantzen used his passkey to enter the kitchen, and they found fruit and pie and helped themselves.

Eating did help, though it did nothing for Garik's life that had been torn away. Basement 1 was overrun with military types and people who looked like everyday workers from Bay City, and Jantzen explained that some of them were, and many of the military personnel were housed on this level, and most of them had no reason to visit the lower levels. When asked why Vang and Wilder were down there, Jantzen shrugged, suggesting they might have been there to observe Garik, and now they were through. Garik thought, good. He wouldn't have to see them again.

They bypassed Basement 2 and went directly to

Basement 3 after eating. Jantzen had someone he wanted Garik to meet, Hector. When the doors opened, Garik was surprised. Basement 2, where his quarters were located, was spacious, with high ceilings, and it seemed it would make a nice place to live, if it weren't a prison. Basement 1 had been almost like outside, with an enormous ceiling. He understood why the climbing wall could extend so high up. Basement 3 felt diminished, like the weight of the entire Corona Tower was pressing down on it, stunting the walls and eating away at the headroom.

Jantzen pointed out how each basement level was smaller than the one above it and the sections that were truncated in comparison to those above. But without any real reference points except his room, the climbing wall, and the elevator, the explanations didn't stick. So what if the top basement level had parking that extended another three blocks in *that* direction, and this floor had only a blank wall? To Garik, it was all impossibly large, and the comparisons were like comparing Jupiter with the sun. When you could fit a million earths inside, all sense of scale was rendered purposeless.

Hector Mascari made more sense. When they entered his massively overcluttered apartment, Garik understood immediately what he had been paired with. He boasted a stiff but sparse mustache, light down over his body, and a very pointed face. He was exceptionally friendly and seemed to take a liking to Garik, shaking his good hand and sniffing of his bandage.

"Very good, very good," Hector had muttered to himself after shaking hands. "Nice boy, friendly boy. Must come visit again." He had moved to the sink, and as he was talking, he scrubbed his hands with hot, running water and soap.

After their visit, once they were back on the elevator, Jantzen casually asked Garik, "What about Hector? What could you tell about him?"

"He had a lot of stuff."

"Fair enough. I should be more specific. He's a failed hybrid—"

"Obviously." Garik pictured the man sniffing his bandaged hand. "He's rat, but he's too much rat, right? That's why he's a failure. You got too much of what you wanted."

"Good guess—"

"Not a guess. The hand washing gave it away. Rats aren't dirty at all, not unless we force them to be." He almost felt sorry for the ones he'd discovered nesting under his aunt's refrigerator, except for the way they'd eaten the wires, forcing him to replace the compressor and causing Arik to come down on him hard.

"Okay, then, not a guess. And yes, getting the correct ratio of DNA has been a challenge, although we're better at it now. Why rat, though? Why would we choose that?"

"They survive everything, better than almost anything else. If the world ends, the rats will still be here, and they multiply quickly. They'll be everywhere."

"Close." Jantzen chuckled. "Cockroaches would survive better, but we haven't attempted that, yet."

"Please say you won't." A cockroach man. It boggled the mind.

"Okay. Then I guess I shouldn't suggest that we might have already done worse."

Garik cut his eyes to him hard. What did that mean? He pictured what he and Marisa had seen on Basement Level 5. Was that what he meant? He was certain he would soon find out.

T

he numbers glowing beside the elevator door shifted from three to two, and the muted steel box eased to a stop like a well-oiled piston. The door released with a ding and began to slip aside, revealing where they had started.

Where Airman Vang had invaded his life and stomped on his day, Garik thought, as he felt his eyebrows crease into a frown. He watched Jantzen pocket the ever-present passkey and nod to him to exit the elevator.

"Back to my cell?" Garik relaxed the lines in his

forehead to hide his irritation. Jantzen Hefferly might be part of his inquisition team, willing to keep the handcuffs on like everyone else, but he hadn't been mean to him—or barked at him when Garik had expressed his opinion. That was a strong plus in the man's favor.

"Remember? Rachel checked you out to me, like at a library." He grinned and chuckled. "I don't have to check you back in until I'm through with you. Are you ready for me to be through with you?"

"Back into a room with four walls and a fake window?" Garik made a disparaging sound with his lips, very near to spitting, which he might if he wasn't inside this very fancy moving box of a floor carriage. He lifted a hand to run through his hair, a familiar gesture from before. When his hand met only the remnants of the curls he'd once worn, it reminded him of everything else that had changed about his life. He glanced around the wood-lined metal box, so nicely finished-out and luxurious. Elevator roulette. Which floor next? Pick and choose, B1, B2, B3, or! Drum roll . . . B5! He had no idea what was on B4, except for the hospital, and only because he had CUT OPEN HIS HAND AND LANDED THERE.

Okay, met Marina there, and that had been a surprise. At least now he knew, and when he escaped, he could let Marisa know.

"So, you're a go for more adventures?" Jantzen

stood patiently, backlighted by the overhead fixtures lining the ceiling outside the elevator. The doors, blocked by his arm, moved as if they wanted to close, dinged, then became flush against the sides once more. Jantzen seemed to be genuinely considering what might interest Garik.

"Amy, is she one of your experiments?" She had done the red route, by Devon's account. The humiliation still stung, and he could feel the final grip he had reached for slipping through his fingers once more, then falling, only to be caught by the safety line.

Amy hadn't needed her safety line. He wondered what she was like. Perfect, like everyone else in this place.

"Amy is someone you will enjoy. I can check if she's available. She lives on your floor." Jantzen nodded his head toward the corridor where a giant B2 testified to the location.

"Okay, if it will keep me out of prison."

"A pretty nice prison." Jantzen turned right, and their feet began to eat up the distance. The corridor was especially spacious after coming from Basement Level 3. He shifted his sleeve, touched his watch, and said, "Rachel, locate Amy for me, please."

Garik didn't hear a reply, but he didn't expect to. His companion likely had an earbud in, which is what he would wear, if they ever gave him his watch back.

JANTZEN HEFFERLY and Amy Howe together were like a flashbang grenade, stunning Garik to the possibilities of what the research in the Corona Tower basement was capable of.

Walking down the corridor from the elevator, Jantzen had touched his ear, paused, and said, "That's fine. We'll meet her there," and he turned to Garik and said, "Want a ride?"

Garik glanced back down the corridor to where the elevator was barely visible, and he said, "Perhaps. I don't know what you mean."

"Sorry." Jantzen shrugged. "I'm throwing a lot your direction on your first outing. This is a big place. Amy is in the gaming center, about five blocks away, if we count by the city above us. We can walk, but if you want a ride—" He let the offer hang in the air.

Garik returned Jantzen's shrug, and the man walked to a wide door, slipped in his passkey, and it clicked, thump, thump, and released. Inside were Segways, Onewheels, a Hovertrax, and others. Even a golf cart, and everything was neatly lined up and plugged in.

"Don't they overcharge? They can't get used that often." Garik touched the handle of the Segway, rocking it back and forth, and knelt at the Hovertrax, wondering if he could control the bright red and black device.

"Safety overrides on the chargers. You might like this."

Garik turned to see Jantzen holding something that interested him even more than the Segway or the Hovertrax. "A ZBoard!" It was an electrically powered skateboard. He recognized it instantly, even though he'd never seen one in real life, and had never hoped to ride one. He reached for it, set it on the floor, and stepped on it.

"You'll need this." Jantzen held out his hand, and in his palm was a black remote control. "Do you need me to—"

"No, I won't." Garik cut him off. "ZBoards don't use them. I've read up on these and watched online instructional videos. I know how this works."

"That's right. The remote is for one of the other types. Anyway, I'm on a Segway." Jantzen thrust the remote onto a shelf, pulled a Segway from the line, and stepped on it. With a whine, it propelled him through the door. Garik pushed off, like a regular skateboard, and he grinned as the board began to carry him along without any effort at all.

With their exit, the door behind them began to swing silently closed. When it connected, the lock secured the devices left inside with a firm double thump.

"Cool," he murmured, no longer interested in the door. Finally, something good about this place, something he could actually do. Too bad Muhammad wasn't here to see him. He was certain he would be jealous as a green bean next to a ball of falafel wrapped in flat-bread.

The gaming center arrived entirely too soon. Garik hardly noticed the way the corridors opened up, the walls turned into individual building fronts, and people began to appear. The sensation of riding the powered skateboard seemed to peel away the fog of despair that had dogged him all day.

The gaming center was a wide doorway into a darkened, flashing cauldron of activity. Jantzen stopped his Segway just outside against a honed steel and bright red wall and stepped off. He waited for Garik to join him, indicating a rack with several other mobility devices.

"Should we lock them up?" Garik was just noticing the people, and several, although not most, were using various powered devices like theirs.

"Everything belongs to Corona Corporation. Nothing to steal. Leave it and follow me."

Garik had expected the gaming center to be a warren of electronics, with virtual platforms, old-style digital arcade games, and even role-playing games. Well, yes, it had all that, but that was just scratching the surface. The real trick was the *people.*

To Garik's eyes, every other person inside was hybridized, and they were doing the *coolest things ever!*

"IS THIS how you people train?" Amy had joined them, and Garik leaned in to talk over the noise of the gaming activities around him—birdlike screeches, the crash of what looked like bowling balls and the fur-covered creatures yelling as they dodged them, a table of drinks knocked over when a hybrid with what must be wings tried to leap into the air and failed, others with extra digits, and a few mutations that Garik didn't know how to describe.

"Training is a floor down, for those of us who need it. We come up here to challenge one another. Besides, it's fun."

Amy was petite, especially compared to the hybrids filling the gaming center, and more than he had expected—having completed the climbing wall *even though she had only done the easy route*, she insisted on telling him. Her hair was streaked yellow and brown, a fashion choice, Garik assumed, and her eyes sparkled with green.

He also noticed a slight buzz when she talked—and then there was her left arm. It was slightly shorter than her right. That hadn't kept her from being effer-vescently friendly when she was introduced to him.

Her big eyes and tiny jaw and mouth gave her an insect-like appearance.

"Don't people get hurt sometimes?" He watched the bird-like man climb off the floor. He didn't seem bothered, and his companions brushed broken glass from him.

"Sometimes," Amy said. "That's part of the fun."

"See there, Garik." Jantzen touched his arm, and he pointed to an elevated ring, like those used for boxing. "This person might interest you. Watch the man in the leather duster."

A man and a woman climbed over the ropes. Lights throbbed overhead, in purple, red, and yellow. Music thumped, and Garik could feel it through the floor. They didn't wear any boxing gear that he could see. Then the man pulled off his duster and revealed incredibly long arms with an extra joint in his forearm. He snapped one arm around, flexing it in a way no normal arm could flex, and suddenly he held a knife.

"How did he do that?" Garik had seen his arm move, but the knife? It hadn't been there, and then it was.

"I'm cheering for Alyna." Amy raised her short arm and called out, "Hoot! Hoot! Alyna!"

"She looks normal—" Garik shot Jantzen a question with his eyes.

"Not quite. Watch." Jantzen twirled his finger for Garik to turn his face toward the ring.

Alyna pulled off gloves, flexed her hands, and she unsheathed massive claws.

"Komodo dragon," Amy breathed. "I should have been so lucky."

The crowd throughout the gaming center had slowly focused on the two participants in the ring. Now that their weapons were exposed, repeated chants calling their names began to swallow the thumping music.

"Is that the man you asked me about earlier?" Garik nudged Jantzen with his elbow. The noise had grown deafening, and they could hardly speak and be heard.

"Justin Kurtew. What do you know about him?"

"Nothing. Dr. Jamie was called away because of him."

"I'm not surprised. He's up from Three. He knows not to bring blood, but with this crowd, who can tell?" With the chanting, Jantzen had become hyper alert, and his eyes scanned the crowd. "Amy, can you help me look?"

"I have been."

Garik looked at her, studying her eyes. She was still focused on the ring and occasionally cheering for Alyna No-Last-Name. In Amy's eyes, Garik caught something else. Each large eye was filled with green crystal structures, each one reflecting something slightly different, as if she could see a hundred different images all at once.

Like a bee, Garik thought, certain he had nailed her hybridization.

A frenzied cheer erupted from around the ring, and Jantzen vanished, his clothes dropping to his chair, and a dark purple smudge flashed through the air between their table and the two combatants in the ring. Garik blinked to see Jantzen's head and shoulders behind Justin Kurtew, with his arms underneath Justin's and holding them up over his head. Justin's hands kept whipping back and forth but were unable to touch anything with his knives, and across from him, Alyna held her forehead, her claws sheathed, and blood seeping from between her fingers.

"He'll want these." Amy sighed and gathered up Jantzen's clothes. "Every time, this is what happens."

"He, um, that was real?" Garik looked from the empty seat and back to the ring, where he could just see Jantzen's dark hair as he helped Justin back into his leather duster. He remembered the video promotion showcasing Jantzen on the mall, the event Arik had forced him to miss. Camera angles and magic fakery, he had thought then. Now, he was thinking, maybe the wrist thing had actually happened.

Jantzen and Amy reappeared, and Jantzen was pulling his shirt over his head. He looked exhausted, but he grinned at Garik. "Not quite the show I intended to offer you, but as you can see, maybe we've done worse than combine a person with a cockroach."

Amy rolled her eyes. "Not that old story again."

"Are all these people, um, like that? You know, that different?" Bloodthirsty, he almost said. The physical differences were a given. They just *were*. "And why were they fighting?" Garik watched Jantzen carefully as he walked around the table and seated himself, just making sure he was as solid as a real person should be.

"That's the reason for the events on the mall. And

probably the reason the good doctor was called away to see Justin." Jantzen looked down to line up a crease on one leg.

"It gives everyone a chance to burn off energy. It's the only time many of them can go outside," Amy added.

"Outside." Garik pictured the tickets no one could seem to get, the twelve-foot wall that lifted from the sidewalks to keep the city folk out, and the light show that simulated the building crumbling into silicon glitter over and over. Wouldn't Marisa love to know how close to the truth she had been?

Had been. *Was.* Marisa wasn't gone. *He* was. She was still just as right as ever.

"Can I go to one?" They had to let him. They must.

"Go to one what?" Jantzen patted his face with a napkin. He was perspiring, and he looked like his vanishing trick had been painful.

"An event. I've always wanted to. Can you get me in?" He had to do this, and before he Houdinied. He might never have another chance.

Jantzen looked hesitant, but Amy said, "Friday night, Jantzen. The Howling Pterodactyls are performing. What do you say?"

"I should say no, but after that exhibition, I don't think much will surprise you. Okay, but you're to stay with me the entire time. No impulsive stuff." He looked hard at Garik's bandage before jumping his eyes back to his face.

"On my honor. I promise." He held up his hand, almost dropped it because of the bandage, then kept it up. "No more of this."

The mall. He would be attending a Tower event, and with Jantzen Hefferly. The Dactyls weren't so wonderful, but to look up and see the silicon glitter tumbling from the sky?

How lucky was that?

— 8 —

G

arik squeezed one eye open and glared at the fake window taking up much of one wall in his room.

Fake window. Fake scene outside. Fake morning sun. At least the blinds were real, even if they only muted the blaring trumpet of the sun's fake rays.

The clapper of the bell at St. Anne's kept going off in his head, and he twisted his face into the pillow, forcing the morning back through the window so he could wrap himself in the comfort of the dark and return to blissful sleep.

He twisted, the sheet binding his legs, and he kicked

his feet, sending the sheet sliding to the floor. His skin prickled in the room's cool air, and he moaned with self-pity.

His night hadn't been comforting and blissful, and that was the problem. Dreams of people with dragonfly eyes, lizard tails, and massive canine teeth had haunted him. He saw Marisa's drawing of Halo Sunchaser slaying a silverback gorilla with her electrified sword, and in the dream, the gorilla had grown larger and larger, smashing the sword and Halo Sunchaser, and then coming after him.

In his mind's eye, the gorilla had become King Kong, a fur-covered Hulk, ever larger, and raging after him. He had jerked awake just as the gorilla's massive hand had wrapped around him and begun to squeeze—

Garik jerked up, sitting, his heart rumbling in his chest like the Bay City trains he sometimes heard at night from his bedroom. They squealed along the tracks to Argyle Station, inescapable, rattling the picture of his parents he kept alongside his bed. Sometimes they caught him unaware in the darkness, and they were an earthquake, about to bring the ceiling down on him.

Garik's nightmare, the gorilla. A silverback, the largest and most powerful of them all. Garik made his way to the window, opened the blinds—squinting at the brilliance slicing into the room—and studied the bird that always flew from the tree outside his parents' rock house. He wasn't warmed or reassured by the scene.

His night had done that to him, and he reached to the side and toggled the selector switch. The scene flickered and became a snow-covered mountain pass, the sky filled with clouds, and falling snow obscuring much of the image. The room darkened. He relaxed his eyes and turned away from the computer-generated scene.

The mall. The Howling Dactyls. Tonight was the night. His heart jumped, faster, although for a different reason. He rubbed his arms, the prickles like sandpaper, the feeling of excitement forcing the traumas of his night into the background.

And with Jantzen Hefferly and his purple mist. He wasn't going to *see* him. He would be *with* him.

He could hardly wait.

ARRIVING AT the event might be the focus of the day but preparing for the evening on the mall promised to consume Garik's time and attention.

Jantzen arrived to escort him to breakfast. He was now regularly eating in the cafeteria on Level 1, sometimes escorted by T'Wana or Van, but today, Jantzen assured Garik he had checked him out "like a book at a library" and they would spend the day together, unless Garik wanted some alone time in his room.

"No way," Garik had retorted. "I'm with you."

Jantzen had laughed. The man was freshly crisp, unlike after his transformation and altercation with Justin Kurtew and his flashing knives. That evening,

Jantzen had offered to give the ZBoard a permanent home in Garik's room, if he wanted.

Two men who introduced themselves as Joseph Howard and Tyrone Brown had arrived the next morning and installed a permanent charging station for the ZBoard. Both men's shirts said Maintenance, but Joseph was the older and came across as the leader. Tyrone smiled a lot, flashing white with his grin. Now, when Jantzen arrived, if he had his Segway, Garik automatically pulled his powered skateboard from the wall. They would be heading on an excursion through the massive basement complex of the Corona Tower, wherever the adventure might take them.

At breakfast on Friday, Jantzen suggested Garik consider the weather for their night on the mall. Today was hot in the real world—meaning summer wasn't yet over—and while it would cool quickly once the sun was down, powerful patio heaters would be set up around the mall. They weren't likely to get cold before the event ended.

Garik wanted to look his best, and with Jantzen's advice, he chose a lightweight, flower print button-up shirt with a black background, dark gray summer slacks, and black loafers. Jantzen arrived at his door in a thin, long-sleeved black pullover with a hood at his back, black gloves, and lightweight black slacks. His black brogues were polished to a shine. With his tight black hair and closely cropped beard, he was transformed into the man Garik had seen so long ago on the food court screens, promoting his upcoming event on the mall. To be here, to be part of it, and with the man himself, was as exciting as Garik thought his week could be.

He couldn't wait to get upstairs—under the stars, if there were any—and be a part of something he had been excluded from his entire life. He didn't know if he would dance like he'd seen people do from his voyeuristic forays from atop his Street Strider, but he was certain he would stand with his arms to the sky as the silicon glitter tumbled around him, and it would be the best night of his life.

Then, tomorrow, he could start in earnest on his Houdini project . . . to get out of this place and back to the life the Tower had stolen from him. He had come to look forward to spending time with Jantzen Hefferly, but that wasn't enough. He missed Marisa, even Irina, if Arik not so much. He hadn't known how much he loved his life until he was inducted unwillingly into whatever they were doing to him here.

He refused to think about the changes he had seen in the people living under the mall in the Tower's basement. He was still Garik. He looked the same, except for his hair. He had been to the activity center with Devon twice, and he sure his body was tightening up. No fantastical teeth, no fur down his backbone, no nothing, except for the bad dreams.

He wanted his life back, but if he had to be here, it couldn't hurt to end it with a night on the mall.

Bam, this could be exciting, and Garik felt it in every fiber of his being.

THEY RODE to the mall, Jantzen on his Segway, and Garik atop his powered skateboard. They passed the elevator they normally used, and Garik did his best to remember the twists and turns to reach the main elevator, the one he and Marisa had ridden the day they dropped into the cesspool he was trapped in. It figured large in his plans to disappear from the Tower's clutches.

Like a Houdini, or a Hefferly. Flash, vanish, and he would be gone.

Garik noted the military personnel at the doors, an extra guard, one at each of the two elevator cars, even with Jantzen's passkey required for access. At the mall level, the elevator doors opened, and they stepped out into the food court. Garik glanced at the food kiosk where he had so many times purchased a drink or fries, surprised, somehow, to see it shuttered. That small moment cemented the difference between then and now. He wasn't stepping back into his old life but living in this new one, even if this was an old, familiar haunt. Around him, the glass walls enclosing the food court were still retracted, leaving the giant glass Tower in its permanent spider mode, hunched on its steel and brick legs, ready to feast on whoever or whatever came within its reach.

It had sure feasted on him, Garik thought dryly, even as his new shirt caught the light breeze and moved across his chest, the touch of the soft fabric reminding him he was arriving first class, unlike what he would have done if Muhammad had been able to land tickets that unlucky morning.

The mall was tantamount with attendees, few of them as tamely dressed as Garik and Jantzen. A military presence was also scattered around the walls and at various places throughout the event. The Dactyls were in full regalia, with their feathered masks and sequin-encrusted boots, and they were tuning their instruments. It was as discordant as if they intended to hurt people's ears, but it was a Rez band, and that's what Rez bands sounded like.

As the music began to come together, Jantzen walked the mall, greeting people, laughing with a few, and introducing Garik to faces he'd never seen. He looked for Airman Wu Han but didn't see him. There were so many military personnel in attendance that he would have been surprised if he had. Of course, Devon was present, with his blond cowlick, but in party mode, with a giant balloon crown topped with a sea serpent. And Amy, in yards of luminescent material, dancing in circles as though flying. Even Marina and Hector. He didn't recognize Marina until she spoke with him. She had on a party mask that covered her eyes, but he knew her voice when she called out to him. Hector seemed to be pickpocketing careless attendees, and Garik understood the reason his apartment looked the way it did.

As the night got wilder and the sky drew darker, Garik kept waiting on the silicon glitter to fall from the sky. Finally, Jantzen asked what he was looking for, and he laughed, explaining that the visual effects didn't extend to those in the mall. They were in a "glitter-free zone." He seemed to find it as amusing as Garik was disappointed.

The names Garik learned that evening stacked up in his mind: Paolo Leveen, with the ends of his fingers in long, claw-like nails. Joanie McDonald, who sported a mohawk. And Julia Cantos, unearthly tall; Giselle Harmon, wearing a pirate mask; Leigh Jose, with her arms crisscrossed with leather straps; and John Carter, who seemed to be a larger-than-life blond god, even fitter than Devon Maye.

At one point, Weston Rodheimer with his broad shoulders and Halo Sunchaser in her headwrap appeared. The excitement of the revelers seemed to diminish when Rodheimer drew near, but they didn't come their direction and left shortly, at which point the noise level and partying ramped back up.

Justin Kurtew was there, but he didn't come and introduce himself. He glared at Jantzen, took in Garik, and walked away. Jantzen pointed out Marco Lopez, wearing a large tail and finding it convenient to climb anything to get a better view. When Garik started to ask, Jantzen shook his head but mouthed, "Lemur."

Garik understood. No discussing DNA mixtures or hybridizations on the mall. There had to be a place where what they had become was normalized. They could be as they were, not specimens to be poked, prodded, and evaluated.

Here, they were normal, because the not-normal ones were like Garik—and Jantzen, Garik supposed, although he could morph into purple mist, even if he looked totally normal otherwise.

Like me, and in that moment, Garik suffered an epiphany of despair. He was no longer normal, or he wouldn't be eventually. What had Jantzen said? He didn't know what changes would accelerate quickly and which would take a while. That meant that Garik wasn't finished becoming whatever he would one day be.

Like these people. His head tightened, and he suddenly wanted to be away.

"Is there a problem?" Jantzen touched his elbow to get his attention.

"I used to think these were costumes. They're not, are they?" Garik's trust in the reality he used to take for granted teetered, his enthusiasm melting into a lump of soul-robbing despondency.

"Most are, but this is where our less favorable transformations can be themselves. Does it bother you?"

"No . . . yes! I don't know." Garik felt the gorilla's hand whipping him back and forth, and he didn't know what he thought any longer.

"Come, I want to tell you something that will help, I think." Jantzen led him under the Tower to a vacant table marked on the top with Chow Down. He pulled out his earbud and turned off his watch on the way. The video screens around the underside of the Tower flashed and sparkled with the Dactyl's flamboyant style. Several people were also taking a break under the tower, but they were nowhere nearby.

"So, what?" Garik felt his Arik voice coming out, and he sat up and apologized. "I'm sorry. I'm just grumpy. What did you want to tell me?"

"Grumpy, maybe, but you have good reason. Your life's been stolen, like mine."

"Like yours?" That caught Garik off guard. This was Jantzen Hefferly. Surely, he liked his life. He lived in the Tower, had power and respect, and he could change into purple mist at any time.

"You noticed the Director didn't come our direction. We've had differences."

"I'm sorry."

"I cared for him once, really cared, before all this." Jantzen motioned to the Tower above their heads and the people dancing in a frenzy on the mall. "I couldn't tell him how I felt, so I supported his research. When his wife died, he changed. Now you see what he is."

"No, I don't see. What is he? He's the boss, isn't he?"

"Much more than that." Jantzen laughed sourly and looked away. "He's like us, you and me, except his transformation, well—" Jantzen paused and cleared his throat, "—maybe that's not the best topic for discussion."

"What? He looks okay to me."

Jantzen tightened his jaw and looked out over the crowd. "Looks can be deceiving, my friend." The man seemed to sink into himself, and Garik had to listen hard to catch his next words, ones he was certain the bearded man didn't intend him to overhear. "For six months I nursed him, thinking he wouldn't survive. Then I begged to be the second trial subject to have something in common with him. Now, it's gone all wrong."

That left him thinking. What's gone all wrong? And how bad could things get? And finally, would it happen to him? He shivered, and he had a patio heater blowing right on him. With the night, it wasn't hot enough to drive away his chill, and thinking about Jantzen's words, he began to doubt that it ever would.

— 9 —

arik's party ended long before the bigger party did.

He and Jantzen sat for a time, Jantzen wrapped in his thoughts, and Garik not knowing how to respond. Out on the mall, people were doing impossible stunts, twisting and jumping, perhaps even flying, although the stunts Garik saw couldn't surely be real. People using drones, or perhaps leaping while attached to wires hooked to the building.

Eventually, Dr. Jimenez appeared out of one of the two elevator cars, pausing as if taken aback by a scene of unimaginable trauma and devastation. Perhaps to him it was. He was still neatly dressed in a hospital jacket, and he even wore a stethoscope around his neck, like he'd just come from the surgical ward.

Or it could have been his costume, but Garik doubted that.

Jimenez looked around, searching, and when he saw Jantzen, he nodded his head, satisfied, and walked briskly their direction. He was almost there when he realized Garik was with him, and he frowned for a moment before replacing it with a smile. Surprisingly, he acknowledged Garik before Jantzen.

"How are you doing, my boy? I didn't expect to see you here. But then, seeing you're with Jantzen . . ." He looked Jantzen's direction and raised his eyebrows.

"Yes, Doctor, he's with me."

"Ah, then I'm not surprised."

"Don't start, Doctor. Now's not the time."

"No, no, I'm sure this is a good thing, get our young man into the gritty undersides of the beast as soon as possible. Does it feel gritty to you, young man? Or are you liking what you see?"

Garik didn't know how to answer, but he could tell there was something going on between them that they weren't saying. He responded in a way that he had mastered with Arik, answering without answering.

"I'm meeting lots of new people." He gave him a smile, knowing the man would expect one.

"A good answer. Now, Jantzen," and Jimenez

turned from Garik, done with him, and addressed the other man. "I'm afraid I have a situation that requires higher authority than mine to resolve. Are you free?"

"I'm supervising Garik. How important is this?" Jantzen visibly pulled himself together. When his eyes passed over Garik, he seemed to fully see him for the first time since their conversation.

"Utmost." Jimenez glanced at Garik, paused, then said, "If you trust someone to take over, I can wait, or we can drop him off at his room."

Garik caught Jantzen's eye and shook his head no, not wanting that almost more than anything, and Jantzen nodded and said, "Let me think, Amy's here, no, let me locate Devon. This is his chance for redemption. He will appreciate that. He didn't deserve his reprimand."

Reprimand. Garik glanced at his hand, seeing the butterfly stitches still crisscrossing the cuts from the glass. He would feel sorry for Devon, but just now he was preoccupied with not being locked up back in his room. He waited, hoping, as Jantzen reinserted his earbud, tapped his watch, and spoke.

"Devon, it's Jantzen. I'm in the food court with Garik. Are you free to supervise?" He paused, then said, "I don't know the situation, so I can't answer that. Thirty minutes, an hour, maybe longer." Another pause, then, "Thanks. Eyes on at all times, Devon. I'll be waiting."

Supervising. Garik narrowed his eyes at the bearded man. He acted like a friend, then he was "supervising." Garik was his "responsibility," to be passed on to someone else. Garik chanted in his head, Eyes on at all times, Devon. Don't let him get out of your sight, Devon. Keep the leash tight, Devon.

And it was all true. He would escape now, if he could. He'd tried it from the other side often enough that he knew the wall was as impermeable as glass to water. He wasn't getting through, not with the wall up, and he wouldn't be allowed out of the basement with the wall down.

Catch-22, it was called. No matter what he did, there was no solution.

Devon showed up, finally, in full party mode, his balloon crown long gone, and his shirt untucked. He held out something shiny and called from fifty feet away, "Look what I found. Will this do?"

It turned out to be a pair of handcuffs, and Garik thought, not on my wrists!

Jantzen laughed, took the cuffs, and clasped Garik on the shoulder. "Do what Devon says. He's helping me out, and more importantly, you're helping him out." He leaned in close and whispered his final words, "For the arm," then he called to Devon, "Remember, eyes on!"

"Gotcha, Mr. Hefferly. Eyes on." Devon tapped under his eyes with two fingers spread wide. Then he laughed. He threw an arm around Garik, gave him a harder-than-necessary squeeze, and said, "This will be fun. Right-o, kiddo?"

Garik shrugged and let himself be dragged into the melee.

GARIK FINALLY convinced Devon to let Amy take him to his room, claiming he hadn't recovered from his "induction" enough, and he felt weak.

Devon dropped his party persona long enough to look into his eyes, put his arm over his shoulders again, and say, "I know how you feel, little man. The party scene is too much for some of us. You'll get here some-day, and that's the truth. Go with God and be a kind person. Okay, kiddo?" He smiled, put his fingers to his lips, blew him a lighthearted kiss, and released him to Amy, before turning back to the festivities and yelling, "Hoot, hoot! Don't be a fruit!"

Anyway, the weakness was true enough, if not exactly the picture he painted for Devon and Amy. The Dactyls were howling, the air had grown cool despite the heaters, and the real problem was that Garik couldn't tell who was real and who wasn't.

Of course, they were all real, but which strange and eye-bending adaptation was part of the person, and which was costuming to disguise what was underneath?

It was like the Tower. He had dreamed of standing in the mall and seeing the glittering Tower crumble around him, and once he was there, it was all a lie, and not just like Marisa's lie. He had expected it was to hide some Tower secret, but to not be there at all once he was part of the inner circle?

Then, Jantzen, all friends, and shuffling him off to another "supervisor" the first chance he got.

Did Amy also hate him? Was she playing happy face and then saying ugly things about him?

Airman Vang was better. At least he knew the man hated him, and he could deal with that.

Inside his room, he listened to the thump-thump of the lock, and it closed him in worse than any lock he'd ever heard before. He peeled his party clothes off, wishing he'd worn something comical or outrageous. At least, people might have laughed at him, like Devon, being crazy just because he could. Devon had been having a great time.

And why wasn't the doctor surprised Garik was at the event when he learned he was with Jantzen? What reputation did Jantzen have? Good? Bad?

And the Director? How was he messed up? And did that mean Halo Sunchaser was something other than she seemed, also?

He found his way to the shower and stood under the hot water, letting it beat at his shoulders. When he knew his skin was red, he killed the water, dried off, and pulled his pajamas from under the sink, slipped them on, and stepped to the "window." It showed nighttime, but it wasn't the nighttime happening just over his head. Even the window was a lie. He toggled the switch to change the view, saw stars, then rain, and finally a city scene, but none of them were of Bay City, no "event" or the Dactyls or the sky that should be above him.

Not even the Corona Tower, continually shattering into silicon glitter and reforming to reveal the finished glass skyscraper ready to be destroyed all over again.

None were of his home.

And he couldn't turn it *off,* just like he couldn't turn his head off. He balled his fist and pounded the wall one time before turning to his bed, falling inside, and hitting the light switch on his bedside table.

By the door, the power connection to the electric skateboard glowed green. It was ready to go play, and yet it had never seen the light of day. Even that was a lie, not a real skateboard, just a toy to chase up and down the corridors inside the basement, following Jantzen, and never turned loose to explore on his own.

Garik squeezed his eyes tightly in the darkness, glad no one was around to see, and he brushed his face with the backs of his hands. He pictured his aunt looking into his room and seeing nothing but an empty bed, Marisa at the flower shop, cutting a fresh arrangement to fulfill yesterday's order, and Robbie on the stairwell, his arms around his latest girlfriend. Did Robbie wonder what had happened to him? Did Irina? Did Marisa?

Or did they all believe the lies, lies, and more lies,

that he was in Russia when he was right here, right where he belonged—except where he belonged was not in the Corona Tower basement. He didn't belong here at all. He was in too deep. How could he ever get out now?

EVEN GARIK'S churning thoughts couldn't keep him awake all night. They could, however, form the groundwork to banish him to a nightmare world as his mind tried to make sense of the things troubling him. That night, he dreamed of the silverback again, a great, hairy beast with eyes that flashed with white light. Laser beams, scorching everything they touched. Garik was more scared than he had ever been, and he knew he could never win against such a frightful opponent.

A black-clothed man appeared, and he pressed something into Garik's hand, saying, "Use it."

Garik held the pommel of a sword, and as he lifted and turned it, it became part of his arm, an extension of his hand, as natural as curling and uncurling his fingers.

The silverback growled, beat its chest, and lifted a boulder that turned into a car. The massive animal hefted the car, locked its eyes on Garik, and chucked the machine into the air.

In his head, Garik heard, "The sword! Now!"

He thrust the pommel into the air, and from the end leaped lightning. It wrapped around the car and held it heavenward, suspended, and doing no harm to anyone at all.

The silverback beat its chest again, howled, and danced from one foot to another. It was furious, betrayed, and intended to make someone pay.

Garik trembled, even as he held the sword that had the power to keep everyone safe. Yet, for how long?

How long could he hold on before the truth came out? He was just Garik, seventeen, weak, and not prepared for this at all. He just wanted to go home.

In that moment of longing, Garik's arm fell, the electrified sword's light and power went wild, and the car fell tumbling to the ground. The silverback beat its chest once more, hooted in triumph, grew ever larger, and with an open fist, ran at Garik, becoming more massive with every step. Its arms were twenty feet long, its fists as big as a house. When the fist wrapped around him and began to squeeze, Garik jerked awake, back in his room and covered in sweat.

He opened his eyes and stared into the blackness, waiting too long for his heart to settle and his chest to stop heaving.

The man in black. Someone had tried to save him. Yet, Garik saw the truth the way it really was. Only one person could save him, and that was himself. And he had failed. He had dropped the sword and let everything come undone.

— 10 —

B

reakfast didn't have the usual appeal the next morning.

Not only was Garik's mind awash with the residue of his dreams, Jantzen appeared preoccupied.

"What?" Garik prodded him, wanting the joking, warm mentor back. He didn't know it until then, but he had come to depend on the dark-haired man as a friend-surrogate. He didn't know if he could ever consider him an actual friend, but he was as close as Garik was getting in this place.

"A situation." Jantzen diddled with his food, cutting his breakfast burrito with a fork, then pushing it back, uninterested. He looked off, scanning the other diners in the cafeteria but specifically not at Garik.

"What?" Garik hit the word hard, and he felt last night's despair rising like bile in his throat.

"Something I have to work out." Jantzen glanced at him, caught his eyes, and turned away.

"What happened last night? That's it, isn't it? What can't you say?"

"How about," and Jantzen let a smile spread across his face, "we give you broader opportunities today?"

"My own passkey?" The possibility sent Garik's heart into double time.

"Not so fast, my little highballer. Passkeys require directorial approval. I am working to get your door unlocked—"

"You can do that? I thought the doors always used passkeys." No passkey, but being able to come and go? The possibility of the unexpected freedom seemed a godsend.

"Only for newbies." Jantzen placed his hand on Garik's wrist, winked at him, and drew his hand away. "I have something else for you today, something you might enjoy. Are you interested?"

"I don't know, but if it keeps me from being locked in my room, probably."

"Hold on a moment." Jantzen stood and walked away from the table, leaving Garik stunned. It was the first time his leash had been unclipped since arriving in this place.

What did it mean?

He watched the man choose a table with several people he recognized from the previous evening. One was the woman with the mohawk, Joanie. He leaned over, spoke with her, and at one point, turned Garik's direction and showed her where he was sitting.

She smiled, nodded, and stood. Two other people stood with her: Paolo, the man with the claw-like nails, and a pretty woman Garik didn't recognize. They headed his direction but, notably, Jantzen didn't.

Again, he failed to see a pattern that made sense to him. These people looked mostly normal, well, as normal as a mohawk and claws could allow a person to be. The third person, well, he would have to wait and see.

Joanie arrived first, carrying a bit of a swagger, and she pulled out a chair roughly, dropping into it. She studied Garik's face as the other two arrived.

"Peach fuzz." Joanie leaned forward, her forearms on the table, and she smirked. "Baby barker."

"Be nice, Joanie." Paolo pulled out a chair and slipped sinuously into it, spreading his hands on the table in front of him as if to announce his differences, the transformation brought on by the mixture of his DNA with another creature. He brought with him a clean, ocean smell.

"Am. Was. Will be." Joanie's eyes were still fixed on Garik.

"What?" Garik spat the word. It was like she was evaluating him, deciding if he was human or not, and his anger jumped to tornado level.

"Joanie," Paolo warned a second time.

"Too human," Joanie said, and she broke her gaze, like she had taken in all the variables, and she had made her decision. She slipped a pack of mints from a pocket, and without looking, slipped one between her lips and made the package disappear.

"Seems like a good thing to be," Garik hurled back. He looked to the third person, trying to place her, and when she put her hand under her chin with her elbow on the table and winked at him, he knew. "Giselle, right?" He had seen her do that to Paolo last night, giving him her rapt attention. He'd wondered if they were a thing at the time, but now she was doing it to him.

"You remember. You are a sweetie, if a bit of a boy." She winked again, and she glanced at Paolo to see how he responded to her tease.

He didn't seem to notice.

"So, what's wrong with being human? I thought that was the plan, to make people who are different but can pass for human." He thought of the scene in the gaming center. Justin's arms and Alyna's retractable claws. Alyna might pass, but Justin, never.

Wasn't that why he was a failed hybrid?

"Pass, not *be*." Joanie turned her head to look back at their previous table. Her mohawk shifted, flexed, and resettled itself where it belonged. Jantzen was gone, but there were others still at the table, watching them, waiting, it now seemed, on Joanie. Joanie jerked her head in a "come on over" motion, and they erratically stood like pop-up toys, gathering their food trays for disposal before heading over.

"More of you?' Garik heard himself adopting Joanie's clipped style of speech. It gave him a bravado he didn't really feel, one he needed to face this over-whelming assault of the Tower's denizens. He recognized John Carter, with his height and blond hair, and Leigh and Julia, but a gothic queen he didn't remember from the night before was new to him.

"So," Paolo began, "what are you?"

Garik was aware of the faces, the new people standing behind the first three, the gothic queen with one elbow resting on Giselle's shoulder, all waiting on his answer.

"I thought we weren't supposed to discuss it." Last night, Jantzen had hushed him. Now, Garik wasn't sure.

"Only at the events." That was the tall Julia. "Down here, no secrets."

Still, Garik thought, why did it matter?

"Okay, baby barker. Already know. For you, I'll squeal. Jellyfish." Joanie didn't exactly smile, but it was likely the closest Garik would get.

Garik laughed. "What's the point in a jellyfish? They don't do anything."

"Except live forever." That was from Julia, and she popped a square of gum in her mouth. Joanie smiled, a real one this time.

"Sea cucumber." Giselle winked and pursed her lips in a kissy-kissy tease.

"And?" Garik wanted to hear this. He didn't think sea cucumbers were good for anything, either.

"I'll show you sometime." Giselle laid a pretty hand on his arm.

"Liquefaction. She can turn to water and back again." Paolo sighed. "It's not a secret."

"I wanted to show him," she pouted. "Besides, I don't really turn to water."

"It looks like it," blond John barbed.

"Tell him yours, then," Giselle vamped, sending him one of her kissy-kissies.

"Wood frog." He looked down as if embarrassed. "I can freeze my own blood and survive in subzero temperatures."

"Thrive, not survive, iceman," Giselle tittered.

"Deal with it, Giselle," John muttered.

"Enough," Joanie barked. "Next?"

Garik's head was spinning. Live forever, turn to water, freezing your own blood? It was craziness!

Still, the revelations continued.

Tall Julia was blended with a boa constrictor. She boasted a built-in infrared heat detector for locating living tissue in the dark.

The gothic queen was Laura Lassere, now half dragon millipede, giving her the ability to breathe out puffs of hydrogen cyanide from specially developed pouches in her throat.

Leigh Jose was part dolphin, though she didn't have a blowhole or the ability to swim underwater for extended periods. She could communicate via ultra-sound, however.

"You," Garik nodded toward Paolo. He looked at the man's hands. "What caused that?"

Paolo lifted his hands and twirled them before smiling. "The remnants of my pinchers. I'm part pistol shrimp."

Ah, the ocean smell now made sense. But pistol shrimp? Garik must have looked puzzled, because Giselle offered a teasing explanation.

"Makes him too hot to touch, if you get my meaning." She winked at Garik even as she placed one hand on Paolo's. Garik noticed that he pulled his from under hers and set it aside.

"I can eject boiling water from my fingertips." He shrugged. "Your turn." He tapped one long fingernail and pointed it Garik's direction.

"Timber wolf." Garik shrugged. It seemed simple and non-evasive, compared to what he had just learned about these people.

"Lucky boy," Julia muttered, looking away, before turning her eyes back to Garik.

"Precog?" Leigh leaned in towards Laura, whispering, but Garik caught her question. Precog, like precognition? That was a wolf thing?

Laura's reply was even more puzzling. "The dog thing hasn't gone so well for Christian, and he's definitely precog."

"True," Leigh nodded. "Seeing the future is seeing your pain."

"Cease!" Joanie stood. "Come." She nodded her head, walked away, and the rest of the group moved with her. Paolo rapped the table, crooked his fingers at Garik, and waited for him to join the group.

Garik scooted his chair back noisily, wondered if he should police his table, and decided there was no time. These people would leave him behind, otherwise.

And he was interested. He wanted to know more.

GARIK'S DOOR double clicked, the thump-thump that told of the lock mechanism releasing.

He was on his bed, still clothed, and too filled with the day to do more than look at the ceiling and try to make sense of everything. Hot water expulsion, sonic communication, and turning to water. What else was possible? Next to those guys, he was nothing. He could hear a little better than before, and maybe his sense of smell was improved, but nothing else. He was still just Garik, Bay City teen on loan from Russia, and living on the struggling side of town. He would never be special like those people.

He wasn't sure he wanted to be. They seemed to have formed a team of sorts, friends, certainly, but they were also skittish about their lives down here, as if their future was uncertain, and they were looking for a way to ensure their survival.

Did he need to worry? It seemed he was being given everything he wanted, even watched over by the second-in-command, a man who seemed to like him and want the best for him.

Jantzen had even gone to bat for Devon when it was Garik who had messed up. Garik still felt bad about that, although there was little he could do to change past events. He would simply have to make better choices in the future.

Jantzen walked in, surprisingly more rumpled and tired than Garik had seen him before. Jantzen smiled, the expression dulled by whatever the day had done to him.

"Hello." Garik sat up. "Thank you for my day."

"I thought you might like them." Jantzen kicked off his shoes, carried himself to the sofa and dropped, leaning his head back. "I'm glad someone had a good day."

"I did. I can't believe all the stuff they can do."

"I can't either, sometimes." His eyes were closed, and he took a deep breath and released it. "What did you pick up from them?"

Ah, a test. Garik deflated. He'd thought . . . maybe

hoped that Jantzen had returned as a friend, and now, he was asking him to evaluate his day, as if the people he'd been with were what mattered, and not Garik or his feelings or what the day meant to him. The disappointment cut, and the thought flashed through him that Jantzen should leave. He didn't need him here, because he was fine on his own.

"Did they say anything?" Jantzen rolled his head sideways and looked at Garik, not irritated or pushy, just reminding him that he'd asked a question.

"They're scared." Garik hadn't thought it just like that, but when it came out, he knew that was it.

"Why? Tell me what you got from them that told you that." Jantzen seemed more interested, as though Garik had noticed something important.

"Their skills aren't good enough." Garik expected Jantzen to agree with him, but the man continued to watch him, not responding, other than a tightened expression around his mouth.

"That's it?"

"No, that's not it at all. They are good, can do amazing things." He thought of Airman Vang, and Colonel Brace from the hospital room flashed into his thoughts. *We've yet to achieve those qualities in a compliant subject.* "They don't play the game, not the way they're expected to. That's what you wanted me to see, isn't it?"

"Last night, I had to initiate a reassignment for one

of our failed hybrids to Basement 5. You know what that means, don't you?"

"Yes." Garik pictured the cages, the mewling creatures, the desperate eyes.

"This one didn't show quick enough progress for Weston, or at least not the kind he wanted."

Progress. Garik thought back to Leah Fortinier's words. *Mr. Rodheimer wants to move this forward.* Airman Vang had been concerned about his lack of progress, also. Then, this morning, Joanie's evaluation. *"Too human."* Garik felt the bile rising in his throat.

"What does that mean for me?" Even to ask it meant it wasn't good.

"That's what I'm trying to work out. Maybe . . . no, it's too early for that. Just know that I'm on your side. I'll do what I can to protect you."

Jantzen stood wearily, sighed heavily, and made his way towards the door. He slipped on his shoes, pulled out his passkey, and inserted it into the lock. Thump-thump, and without looking back, he was gone.

Garik pulled his knees to his chest and wrapped his arms around them. Try to protect him?

He didn't feel better, not any at all.

an Hermoso was the first one in Garik's door the following day.

"Good morning, Garik." He smiled too broad of a
smile, as if he hoped to cover up something he didn't
want to say. "I see you're up and dressed. T'Wana will
be joining us for breakfast. We have a full morning
scheduled for you, so you'll be getting a break from
your room this morning. How does that sound?"

"But . . ." Garik held his hand over his computer
keyboard in the middle of typing a search query.

"Go ahead, shoot. I'm listening." Van smiled, but

Garik noticed it was a little less broadly than before.

"I have a full morning already scheduled." He motioned to the computer. It was on and connected to the research center's educational site. He was expected to keep up his studies, even though it seemed irrelevant with being locked away in this basement PROBABLY FOR HIS ENTIRE LIFE. "And this afternoon, Devon said I could spend some time climbing with him. Can't this wait?"

"I'm afraid not." Van walked to his closet, opened it, and pulled out a pair of athletic shoes. "Excellent! These should do. If you will get these on, we'll head to breakfast. Get you all sorted out, all that stuff. I wouldn't plan on making it to Devon's, but we'll see closer to lunch. T'Wana will update you with more information at breakfast."

"Okay." Garik shrugged. He didn't mind missing the school lessons, but his climbing lesson with Devon? That was less comforting. And Van's overly upbeat attitude? It was like leading a puppy to the pound and repeating, "Here, puppy. Good puppy." It sounded nice, but the results wouldn't be agreeable.

Rather than argue, Garik worked his feet into the shoes and stood. He touched his keyboard to bookmark his place and shut it down. He had pants and a shirt on and nothing else to take with him. He glanced longingly at his ZBoard, but Van liked to walk everywhere, so the skateboard wasn't an option.

Both T'Wana and Van joining him for breakfast? The bad vibes were off the chart, and Garik wondered how his life would be different after today.

GARIK REACHED the side of the pool, barely, and pulled himself far enough out of the water that he could breathe. His chest heaved, and he expected the volcanic upheaval in his stomach to breach the levee as soon as he quit wheezing. He was fully clothed and had been wearing a pack with weights on his back *for twelve laps of the pool.*

Were they trying to kill him?

All morning, he had sat in a room on Basement Level 3 guessing what was on cards, prompted by a band wrapped around his arm that gave him a mild shock with each wrong answer. They kept upping the shock value with each question.

His success rate had been nearly nil.

He guessed Leigh and Laura didn't know as much about Christian as they thought. Precog? There was no such thing in Garik's brain, and he had the scorch marks on his arm to prove it.

Rapid reading skills, flashing words in front of him until they blurred. His head had been spinning before they finished. Then he had been placed in a maze, inside a soundproof room, he thought, because it had gone deadly silent when they closed the door. Inside was a full-size, walled-in maze, and once he was inside, they had turned out the lights. It didn't stay quiet. They expected him to find his way out WITH REZ MUSIC BLASTING THE ENTIRE TIME.

He left that one with his head splitting open.

The pool was the culmination of sprints, one after the other, chin ups that required his chin to reach past the bar, two-minute non-stop crunches, and a full minute of pushups. He had to restart three times on the pushups, each time more exhausted and more determined to finish than before.

Airman Vang and Colonel Brace had shown up during his weight training test, and they had a phalanx of six others with them, one of which Garik thought might be Wu Han, the Airman he had met in the food court. He didn't understand the reason for the basketball throw or the kettlebell snatch. He hadn't even known there was such a thing as a kettlebell snatch, and he dropped the heavy weight several times before he got the hang of it, and with everyone watching, to his mortification.

Dr. Jimenez was there the entire time, with Nurse Ratchett, observing, marking things down, occasionally saying just loud enough for Garik to make out, "Enough, gentlemen. We don't want to kill him."

Thank you, Garik thought, though he didn't expect it was out of personal concern for his welfare. More likely, they didn't want to have to carry his dead body out of wherever he expired. If he was alive, he could walk out and die on someone else's time.

After they watched Garik pull himself from the pool and shuck off the weighted pack, kneeling and trying to figure out why he wasn't dead already, Dr. Jimenez appeared with a tablet and a stylus and directed him to a bench off to the side.

"Come, my boy. We're learning much today. Let's have a seat over here."

"Garik," he growled. "I'm not a boy. I'm me."

"So I see. Let's sit and have a talk."

"Sure." He was sopping, his shoes were filled with water, and he'd completed twelve laps of the pool. How about you, Dr. Jamie? Want to give it a try? Still, he stood, walked as steadily as he could, gently lowered himself to the bench.

"Did you see the Colonel earlier?" Jimenez sounded kinder than Garik had expected.

"Yes." Garik used his hand to wipe the remnants of pool water from his face.

"And Director Rodheimer, did you notice him?"

Garik hadn't, and he looked up and across to the observers at the far side of the pool.

"Oh, he's gone, now. I dare say he's not impressed with your progress."

"What's not to impress? I completed everything you people gave me to do. What do you want from me??"

"Clearly, more than you're giving us. We expected much more from you by this point. It seems the DNA enhancement hasn't taken with you as expected." The doctor seemed almost wistful.

"So I can go home?" If so, the tests today were worth it, just to get out of here.

"Oh, you misunderstand me. No one who starts the program ever gets to go home. You are a permanent part of the facility's residents. There are, um, other avenues for your skills, those you are able to maintain."

Like Marina and Hector. They got more than they wanted from them, and now they were useless to them except as grunt labor. What was Garik, less than useless? He still had his arms and legs. He could run, jump, and swim. Wasn't that worth something?

Would he end up like Devon, instructing those who might show prospective skills? Or like T'Wana or Van, nudging other inductees, unwilling or otherwise, into the best their newly hybridized bodies could be?

"Can I change into dry clothes?" Enough was enough. For once, Garik could be locked in his room for two days and he wouldn't care.

"Let me ask you this, Mr. Shayk. Do you have anything else to give us? Are there reserves in there you haven't tapped, yet?"

Garik heard the man's words. Mr. Shayk. He had been demoted to a last name. If that didn't mean he was on the way out, what would?

"I'll all used up, Dr. Jimenez. I don't have any more to give you."

The man jerked his head up at the use of his last name. He started to say something and instead hardened his jaw and took a deep breath.

"Then, Mr. Shayk, you may get into your dry things. Put all this away first, so that Devon doesn't have to." Dr. Jimenez stood, adjusted his lab coat, and with firm steps, walked away without looking back.

GARIK SET the plastic bag with his clothes on the counter in the changing room. Rooms, because there was space for twenty people or more. It was all his, today.

The sound was as muted in here as it had been in many of the other rooms, and he suspected it was sound dampened and insulated so that whatever happened in here never made it past the door. That was as unnerving as everything else that had happened to him since arriving here.

What could happen in here that needed total secrecy? How bad could it be?

He left the wet clothes in a pile in the corner. He had policed the outside equipment. They could carry this away. He worked his dry clothes on, looking at his arm before slipping his shirt over his head. The red whelps from the glass hadn't disappeared, not quite. He was surprised how quickly it had healed. Even the butterfly stitches were only on for days. Shrugging, he pulled his shirt over his head, worked his arms through the sleeves, then pushed the sleeves up to his elbows. At the bottom of the bag was the passkey they had given him. Van had said it only worked the one elevator from Basement 3 to Basement 1. Breakfast to training, the two places he was trusted to go.

And access to knock on everyone else's door on Basement 2. He knew some people now, and with this, he could look them up, maybe even make some friends. Perhaps even Houdini out of here someday, although the chances of that seemed to be getting slimmer and slimmer.

He thrust his hands into his pockets as he charged out of the changing room, angry at the Tower, angry at the doctor, angry at the turn his life had taken, and especially at his helplessness to do anything about it. As the door slammed back, hitting the wall and echoing into the vast space surrounding the pool, he was surprised to see a familiar person leaning casually against one wall, his feet crossed at the ankles, and his arms crossed at his chest.

Jantzen unwound himself and said, "So, how did it go?"

Garik's throat filled up, his eyes filled up, and he fought to keep his face straight. Worse than awful, he wanted to say, but he was afraid he would fall to pieces if he did.

"That bad, huh? Well, I have some people who might like to spend some time with you. Do you think you, maybe?" Jantzen held out a hand, palm up, and crooked his fingers. He began to back away, leading Garik somewhere, who knew where.

Garik felt a grin break on one side of his face. He sniffled, shook his head yes, and pressed his shoulders to his eyes. Yes, he knew there were wet crescents, but the suddenness of Jantzen's unexpected invitation was a surge of warm molasses covering his bitter interaction with Dr. Jimenez.

Maybe he did care. He was here, wasn't he?

Garik kept his head tucked, and he still sniffled, and his hands were thrust deep into his pockets, but he wasn't alone, and right then, that counted for everything.

— 12 —

T

hey exited the natatorium, leaving the shimmering pool behind, and passed by a dining hall—smaller than the one on Level 1—where the lights were on, but only a few tables were occupied. Jantzen waved, called out to two people named Heath and Chad, neither of whom were familiar to Garik. Chad was in a motorized chair and appeared to be disfigured in a way Garik couldn't define.

Several tables away, Justin Kurtew sat alone, this time in a tight shirt, revealing more differences in his physique than Garik had noticed in the gaming center.

He was hunched over his table, his back especially long and convoluted, and his arms with their extra joints rapidly reordering the pieces of a game, also unfamiliar to Garik. He glanced up at Jantzen and Garik, his face darkened, and he went back to reordering his pieces without speaking.

"He's in a bad mood." Garik's hands were still thrust into his pockets, but he was interested in their destination. They had already bypassed the elevator, and he couldn't make sense of why.

"Justin hasn't dealt well with his slot in the program's hierarchy. He was too early in the program for us to have the kinks worked out."

"The reason he got the arms." And they had been too cautious with Garik, and he had gotten nothing, nothing worth crowing about. That would be fine, except now he would be locked away in this place forever with nothing to show for it, not even a deadly weapon he could use to display his massively successful combat skills, always at the bottom of the totem pole.

No one would ever bet on Garik because he was nothing worth betting on.

"Yes, but mostly he hasn't come to terms with his new self. That's a parameter only the volunteers in the program can control."

"He volunteered?" Garik recalled several comments he'd overheard suggesting people wanted to submit to the DNA melding process, but he'd not put it together that someone would choose to be changed into something so not normal.

"Most of our hybrids have." They had walked some distance to the area near where they had visited Hector Mascari. Jantzen stopped at an unlabeled door. "That surprises you, doesn't it? I hadn't considered that."

"Even the rejects."

"The hybrid failures, yes. They are the ones that live around here. They know the risks when they join the program." Jantzen had out his passkey, but he hadn't inserted it.

"Like Christian."

Jantzen's eyebrows went up. "What do you know about Christian?"

Garik pushed his hands deeper into his pockets. Stupid Garik. Saying things without thinking. It was his ears, hearing things people hadn't meant for him to know.

"Spill the beans. Has someone been talking to you about Christian?"

"Will I be sent to Level 5, too?"

"What?" Jantzen's passkey disappeared, and he grasped both of Garik's shoulders. He looked him hard in the face. "What's this about?"

"They said—"

"They?" Jantzen's purple-flecked eyes bored holes into Garik, searching as though he could reveal the answer he wished to hear by intent alone.

Garik couldn't tell, not if it would get Leigh and Laura in trouble. He remembered Devon and his reprimand, so he repeated his previous word, spitting it hard to ensure the man accepted it as all he would get. "*They* said he was combined with a dog. A wolf is like a dog, and I think he's in the cages down there."

"Okay, I don't need to know their names. It must have been someone in Joanie's group. I didn't expect them to be so careless."

"They weren't." Garik wanted to kick himself. "I overheard it, and they didn't know I could."

Jantzen sighed. "Accepted. I forget that you can do that. What else did they say? Anything I need to hear?"

"Did Christian have precog?"

Jantzen released Garik's shoulders and closed his eyes for a moment. "Not had, still has. He's alive and well, just up for reassignment. You're going to meet him tonight." His passkey reappeared, and he pushed open the door, revealing blaring music and flashing lights on the other side. Marco Lopez was hanging from the ceiling holding a bouquet of flowers and chewing on a yellow carnation.

Garik burst out, "What?"

"I thought you would say that." Jantzen grinned. "This is Christian's apartment. Hurry before we draw attention." He pulled Garik in and closed the door behind him.

"CHRISTIAN MAGUIRE." A tall man with black eyes inside deep blue, and those surrounded by lighter blue, like those of a husky, peered down at Garik with his hand held out to shake. He was shaggy and tousled, with coarse hair that didn't look as though it would accept a comb. His outsized arms and legs gave him a playful, boyish appearance. His rough-knit sweater was littered with wisps of hair that matched that on his head.

"Hello, Christian." Garik felt overwhelmed, even more so than when discovering Justin's crazy arms or Alyna's retractable claws. The man seemed friendly enough, but his size was daunting. When he shook, Garik's hand was swallowed in the man's big paw.

Paw. The thick hand did resemble a paw. He wondered how long it had taken the man's hand to change from normal to that, and if his own would someday look the same.

The apartment was small, one room, about the size of Garik's, and everyone he knew from the project was crammed inside, the hybrids he'd befriended, anyway. The non-hybrids—Van, T'Wana, Devon—were off doing whatever they did, which was likely something very non-hybrid. The room did have a small kitchen, which Garik didn't have, but no bed. Instead, cushions filled one corner. Marco had returned to the floor to pilfer more flowers, before leaping to the top of the doorframe. He was now perched on a handhold Garik couldn't even see.

"I thought you were, um—" Garik wasn't entirely sure *why* they were here. He hadn't expected to meet Christian, and for everyone else to be here?

"Reassigned? Not yet. Jantzen is working on a solution."

"I don't understand why everyone's here. They are, like, having a good time. How, I mean, I guess I'm asking, shouldn't everyone be sad?"

"Give Jantzen time. He will explain." The oversized man had bypassed the couch for the floor and sprawled like a large pet. He rested an arm and his head on a cushion and nodded his head at the people eating, drinking, and laughing at each other's antics. "They're here for support."

"Okay." A farewell party? No one seemed especially concerned that the man would soon be assigned to one of the cages on Basement Level 5. "Are parties like this allowed?"

"Not forbidden, but yes, we would be in serious trouble if they knew why we're here." Christian seemed amused. "We won't be, though."

"How do you know?" After today, Garik didn't need more trouble. What would happen, another twelve laps in the pool, this time with bricks in his pack?

"I can see it, twelve hours out."

"Your precog ability." Garik closed his eyes. He had done it again. He wasn't supposed to know.

"They hope for better in you."

The tests that morning with the cards suddenly made sense . . . the electric shocks on his arm . . . all motivation for him to make the right connections.

"Unlucky them. I'm not anything."

"I know. Not yet, anyway." Christian nodded as if it was obvious.

"How—" Garik stopped. Christian looked at him with an *are you kidding* roll of the eyes. "Precog, right. I didn't know you could tell things like that about other people. I thought precog was about what happened to you."

"And here you are telling me this." Christian pointed. "There's our friend. I'm glad we got to talk."

Garik felt Jantzen at his side. The bearded man clapped him on the shoulder, nodded at Christian, and leaned in and said quietly to the big man, "Give me time, my friend," and motioned to Garik to follow him.

They headed across the room to where Joanie was having a spirited conversation with Alyna. Whenever Alyna moved her hands to make a point, the tips of her claws extended, like a cat when flexing its paws, only these were daggers that could slice like razors. Garik noticed a flash of silver in one of Joanie's hands and realized she was popping mints like candy.

Giselle was at Paolo's elbow, watching him with adoring eyes, and Laura, by that time, was yelling at Marco to BRING BACK HER DAISY! IT WAS

DECORATION FOR HER DRINK!

"Why has he given up?" Garik couldn't believe they were all having a good time when a friend was about to be sent off to whatever would happen to him on Level 5. He had been there. He had seen the results in the cages. He glanced back at Christian to see several others had gathered around him, and they were making the man laugh.

"He hasn't. That's his nature. Kind, generous, quick to warm to strangers. It's also why the military doesn't need him."

"Military?" *Stop repeating people*, Garik scolded himself.

"You haven't seen them?" Jantzen gave Garik a mock stare.

"Sure, yes. All the time when my friends and I were at the food court. But what do they have to do with Christian?"

"This I'm surprised you don't know. That's where our money comes from, the military."

"Oh. That's why I've seen so many uniforms going into the Tower."

"You never put it together?"

"No." Garik shrugged. "I never had any reason to."

"Exactly what they intend. Any other questions?"

Garik looked back at Christian. "What will happen to him? The things I saw down there were broken-down leftovers. Christian's a person. Can't he live here like

Justin and Hector?"

"He's considered more valuable for genetic material. For research purposes." Jantzen looked around the room at the group of genetic hybrids interacting with one another as if evaluating their worth against Christian's. "He's not the first to be scavenged for body parts. That's what the research is about. We're building better soldiers, an army that can out-think, out-maneuver, out-kill any enemy that comes our way."

"No!" Anger surged through Garik. It wasn't fair, not for anyone. To think of a man being sacrificed for that, even if he barely knew him—

"That's how I hoped you'd feel, why I invited you tonight. You can help if you will. After this morning, you might be Christian's salvation."

"I don't see what you mean." His *disaster* of a morning? How could that help?

"Are you willing? That's all I need to know."

How could he refuse? Garik jerked his head in a quick nod.

Jantzen grinned. He interrupted Joanie's animated conversation with Alyna. "Joanie, I think we have a willing helper."

"For Christian? Rockin!" Joanie pumped her fist. "He deserves all the help he can get."

"Eh, eh, e-hay, little man! First time to meet. I'm glad to have you on the team!" Alyna reached to take his hand, her claws disappearing just before she grasped his palm to pump it enthusiastically. "It's gonna be a fun ride!"

"Team? What ride?" Garik looked around, now suspicious that this gathering was less about Christian and more about him. What had he joined? And did he want to be part of it?

Jantzen held up a hand, and he explained, "I told you Weston and I have had some differences."

"You and Mr. Rodheimer when we were on the mall. I remember." Garik saw Jantzen's eyes harden.

"It's bigger than that. Too many people are being cast aside in his quest for perfection—"

"Yeah, us," Alyna called, pumping one arm. "Down with the oppressor!"

"Not too loudly," Jantzen cautioned.

"Who can hear us in here?" She grinned gleefully. "Turn up the music!"

"More seriously, he needs to be pulled off his pedestal and given time to rethink the goals he's pursuing."

"Okay, but what about Christian?" Rodheimer's pedestal wasn't Garik's concern. The thought of Christian being cast aside for *research* was. The man might be a new acquaintance, but they also shared canine DNA. What happened to Christian could as easily happen to him.

"Go ahead." Jantzen encouraged him to continue.

"Christian can't be sent down to the cages. He just

can't. You've got to rescue him." He didn't add, *and me.*

"We have a plan. And that is why we need you. You're still with us?"

"What do I have to do?" Garik let his eyes skip from face to face, his heart filling his chest with anticipation and dread. He thought of the bricks if he were caught.

"Play a lie, at least until it becomes the truth."

"Play a lie—" Garik squeezed his eyes shut. *No more repeating people.* Still, a plan, and they needed him. He looked across the room to Christian reclining next to Marco the lemur man, thinking about what might happen to the big man if he didn't help and the consequences if Garik's lie were discovered. He nodded. "I can do that." *And swim with bricks if need be.*

Jantzen leaned in. "Here's what we're asking you to do . . ."

In Book Three, Garik Shayk must find a way to escape
The Human-Hybrid Project.

The Mirror Cracks
Book Three
The Human-Hybrid Project

Garik Shayk faces the ultimate challenge. His body
is changing, into what final form, he doesn't know. He
sorely misses his girlfriend, Marisa, certain she thinks
he has abandoned her. When Garik makes his break for
freedom, the Tower sacrifices everything to bring him
home. Bay City might not survive, but Garik will fight
back at any cost.

The Human-Hybrid Project

Addictive!

A 10-book series you won't be able to forget. Explore each upcoming book, the characters, and more at www.thehumanhybridproject.com.

Book 1   Book 2

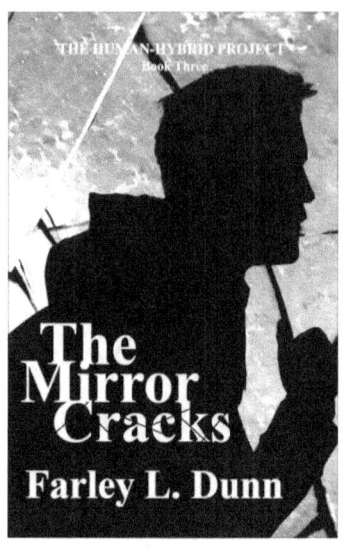

Book 3

Book 4

Book 5

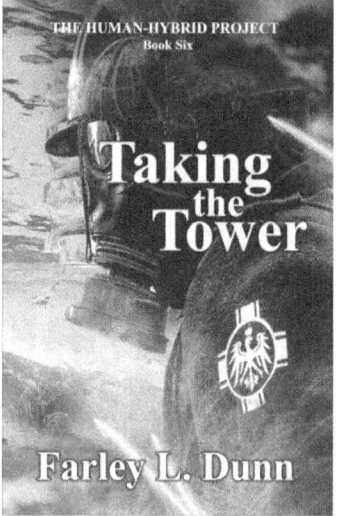

Book 6

Book 7

Book 8

Book 9

Book 10

www.ingramcontent.com/pod-product-compliance
Lightning Source LLC
Chambersburg PA
CBHW070555180626
46817CB00005B/1849